I0538337

Chapter One
Gentleman

It's as if he were dreaming. He is an embodiment, the epitome of pity. The faint light of dawn brought along those feelings of nostalgia and regret that he has become accustomed to. A reality, without knowing that it is reality. In one fell swoop, the world became a place of chaos. It levitates above him, the eyes of a God, one that has forsaken him for the last time. Eyes hollow, but only in a spiritual and emotional state. Head hung low, not from shame, but from an ominous, omnipotent manifestation of unanswered inquisitions and repressed recollections that emanate against the background of perpetuality of time and the physicality of this current realm of existence. Blanched hands tremble in place within the lifeless, stale air of his surroundings. He takes a deep breath, inhale, exhale. The cigarette burns slower, the gentle sounds of crackling tobacco and paper, faint as ever. It rests between his fingers, its smoke entwined with the dust, illuminated only by faint, piercing rays and flickers of sunlight, creating the most intricate and dreamlike state of melancholy within the arms of the hellish prison of memory. Let go. The end of the cigarette marked the end of his day. Vision begins to slowly blur, splitting surroundings into an incongruous symmetry, a little too much whiskey, he believes. He waits for her to caress his arm and guide him back into the house, the sound of her voice permeating through the smoke of the cigarette, his passion as a backdrop of nonchalance, the breath of harsh whiskey, dreams of a hazy, disenchanted frolic. She is not there. Passions, dreams, overcome by stagnation, addiction. Neither remedy nor cure could ever be strong enough to subside the immense conflict and emotion that subsists within the disappearance of his wife. He contemplates the horizon. If he can gather the courage, he can leave such darkened reality to create a brighter destiny, just beyond the edge.

Nine months, two weeks, three days have passed since her sensuous, luscious voice kissed his conscience to sweet serenity. He cradles his head in his hands, vociferating a resonance that only the walls, the ceiling, the floorboards can discern. Her disappearance remains to be solved, forever anguished and absorbed as one moment entwined within his very core of being, void of fortitude and coherence. Memories fade in and out, radio transmissions from times past vaguely resembling brief still frames amidst the wave of perpetual signals of time. Dreamy, his reality seems to be, the way every choice or action feels guided only by fate, without the reprieve or thought towards what happens next. It's all happening. He has no chance to breathe. In between time and space, as he defines them, his wanderlust of wonder swells to encompass all that surrounds him. Sullen eyes and sunken hearts anchor him to the past as the vast palette of emotions permeates and breathes heartless life into the walls of his house and the bars of his prison. At one point in time, reality was fixated, stagnant, but only in the sense that it was tangible. It all ended. There is no solace to be found here. These walls have become the willing witnesses in the gutting, the disembowelment of the soul of a man. An insertion of a knife in his stomach. Jagged edges pulling apart the stitching of the mannequin of existence. The bloodletting starts, organs exposed to an unfamiliar environment as they fall to the ground of what was once a home.

I will always love you.

Change. He ponders the changes that have occurred. Her disappearance transgressed the criterion of the depth of motions that can readily and easily be transcribed or canvassed. Her disappearance paralleled his immersion into alcohol, a sour comfort that allows him to revel in the sweetness of times past. This is how he has lost his way. There is no other way. Take away the soul, the heart of a man, and what is left? James Covington. A damaged, ruined shell of a once prominent gentleman. An educated man, with connections in high places, the places that mattered the greatest, not only to himself, but with his community. He was a captain by choice, a master of the ocean, single-handedly responsible for reviving the fishing industry and town of Noumena. At this time, wealth was abundant and happiness was equally embraced by every citizen in town. Noumena was a prime paradigm, an admirable exemplar of how egalitarianism and utilitarianism conduced a certain utopia of sorts, one where each citizen was uniformly enraptured with the notion that the best was yet to come, while pretermitting to count their blessings for how things have been. In this sense, the past was perfect, such an idealized disguise.

Its history of its becoming was not as bright as its aspirations, though. The ocean was not as cooperative as before, and abundance was not a word to be whispered from the lips of disappointed fishermen and their families. Decades of destitution followed, claiming the dreams and lives of many that dared to challenge the ocean at her own game. What used to be thought of as the best location to establish an industry of fishing was quickly proven wrong, and depression seeped through the cracks of the ceilings of desolate buildings and homes and passed imperceptibly between the fingers of dreamers and those that held onto the hope that change will come. Many have perished out in the ocean, and a mural stood freely in the middle of the town, a testament to those lost, and those that would eventually join them amongst the recollections of all around. As fate would have it, hope prevailed and the tides changed to gently push the residents of the town into the spotlight of good fortune and long awaited blessings, as the currents of the ocean opened its arms to blindly embrace the fishermen and the chaos they would soon invocate. Always remember, nothing lasts forever.

James had made quite the reputation for himself as a fearless navigator of the treacherous Coane Ocean, reeling in cheers of astonishment every moment he would set foot on the shore with the eye of the storm behind him, calmly awaiting its instance to unfurl its cruelty upon him, smothering his listless body amongst dark waters, downward into depths unknown. Bravery and triumph became the bloodline of Noumena, but with every trial of luck comes incongruous tribulation. Discordance always seemed to fall upon the town as an ensemble, harsh and drastic, always uprooting the steady foundation and allowing gravity to entertain its fall back to bitter reality. James had become an idol, a symbol of perseverance and optimism, a certain outlook that Noumena became accustomed to. His pride became an entity, overpowering the might of waves and her lashings. The darkness of the ocean, the void of unbecoming was no longer a threat to other fishermen, as their eyes witness the exuberance and courage emanating from James and the way he effortlessly suppresses the raging beast. Time then became a blur.

Chapter Two
Time

Time is confined within a spectrum of dimensional ranges, varying within and without an individual being, and in essence, is defined by the inevitable end of the aforementioned ranges, where one can possibly fathom what's further, but its implausibility is restrictive, as if a mental obstruction inhibits the progression of the development of advancement towards the attainment of a supposed enlightenment. The expanse between dreams and reality are as infinite as the vacuum of space, as are the possibilities of endlessness, a place, time, and sense of pure bewilderment that is able to transcend further beyond what our imagination allows, in only a perceptual and sensual essence. Abstract it is not, as parameters are placed, the ones that are imposed by self and cognizance. Perceptual it is not, as the sense of sight, in essence, is of a physical and tangible disposition, where the abstract and the imperceptible must be reconstructed to adhere to the boundaries of time within the mind and the physiological domain imposed through five primary senses. Time radiates through every motion that stirs from the body, the gentle, caressing hands of fate guiding time and the individual along in a manner that is perpetual and simple, complex yet necessary. Memory, in instances such as this, can form and thrive to be the brightest cloud in Heaven, or the darkest, cavernous depths of Hell. It can be the feeling of ecstasy, the free fall into the past at the pace of euphoria, or it can be the torrential bars of the prison of time, where one can reminisce over what may have been, but forbidden to cross the threshold of the present pain and agony, forever to be anchored to the strongest tendon in the feet, never to attempt an escape from the constant realization of one's past. Such feeling and feat it is, to try to change the outcome of what has transpired, such perfection of vision that is obtained after such turn of events. Regret not over what has happened, how events came to be.

Regret is a prison, like time, that will snare the limbs in complete, isolated suspension over crystalline pools of what may have been, what dreams may have deviated from memory. Time is chronology, an order of events. As real or unreal as it may seem, it does exist, yet its attributes or dimensions are not limited to what is perceived in the physical realm. Perhaps a memory is an overly meticulous imagination. But then again, after fifteen years of marriage, hardly anything seems to be an imagination, and memories become more real as time passes, especially after calamity and dysphoria. Enough memories were made to last a lifetime and beyond, but life ended for James. Nine months, two weeks, and three days ago.

Chapter Three
Translucent

Life was once wondrous, with a loving wife, an enjoyable career, and sturdy roots that bound him to Noumena. All was well until once upon a tragic time, the loving wife was tersely removed from the triptych of his existence. Such anguish that can come from such love! Everything can change from abruptness, as quick as the blink of an eye, a recurrent theme and moment that builds upon itself the framework of a perfectly symmetrical dream-like euphoria or a finely splintered reminiscence of an aching, vivid nightmare. Human senses reach a heightened level of awareness and forgetfulness when flirting with emotions or stimuli that crosses the threshold of what humans claim to be the radiant glow of repetition, or familiarity. Look below to see what's above, peer within to illuminate what's without. Without seeing so, what's within may withhold and withdraw. Exposure, the undressing of a virgin with worrisome eyes, the faint grip of what feels material before closing the palm of a hand against the wind, against redundancy, disillusion, and false reprieve.

Noumena is back to what it used to be, a small, deserted town of the ghosts of past residents. Buildings wither without respite, the calm breeze of the ocean as the unlikely culprit. The residents vanished. The only other person that resides in Noumena lives two miles away, his neighbor, a fellow fisherman who gave up the ocean for the woods. A natural born hunter, this man used to proclaim, just not of the ocean. He put the importance of his job and the pride of his community before his wife and children, not aware of the consequences of his act. His family left him. Not enough attention being paid to the needs of a growing family. He regrets much, but has moved on. Something James cannot do. The remainder of the residents left before the fishing industry collapsed. In tight knit communities such as Noumena, religion can easily become the backbone and foundation of its residents. Puppets of religion would easily express vexation over the omens of God, warnings to the whole of humankind to better take care and nurture the environment for fear of spiritual reprisal and condemnation. Over time, fanaticism spread, such a contagious virus, and logic and reasoning was left to the wolves, which there were plenty of. James remained, despite witnessing the disintegration of the lifeline of the town, the sustainability of the lives of the residents. Ever since she disappeared though, he has not figured what to do, to stay with the memories of his past, or to follow blindly with the hope of a brighter future. The former chains him to whiskey and cigarettes, that familiar feeling of intoxication. The latter he only experiences when sober, when the realization that his silent audience has had enough of the misery, the bruised knuckles against the walls, the empty bottles of alcohol shattered across the kitchen floor, the last-second decisions to lower the gun from his head. He ponders how perhaps one day, the courage to overcome the past and walk the first step towards a brighter tomorrow can become plausible, so long as the past does not outstretch its fading hands over aspirations of what's present. He wonders if he is strong enough to make that choice. Which decision though remains yet to be decided. He ponders whether his will is strong enough to make the journey to the edge of the horizon, the same one he sees every evening through bloodshot eyes, to dismantle the present and to repair. The end of the road of resentment and anguish can easily be met through a simple movement of his finger on the trigger.

Such odd creatures humans are, having come so far through the conquest of vast terrains of land and technology, yet afraid of the simple process of death. It's as natural as life, yet we fear the unknown. The unknown keeps him in place, the anchor that weighs him down each day, heavy enough to affect his every decision pondered. Quite frankly, he is a creation of his own demise, his own fear. A slave to his own destiny, his own self. Such is life, we create the knitting of the fabric on which our heads rest upon in the end. We shall reap what we have sown.

He is slow to standing, careful not to fall over. It's getting late. He glances at his addiction. He feels weak, and decides to keep the bottle in one piece. He walks through the door, hands brushing along the wall to support him, physically. Floorboards creak, revealing the age of the house. Fragments of glass crack under his shoes, a sordid reminder of previous nights. Once again, a familiar set of words formulate in his thoughts. Perhaps tomorrow won't be so bad. And at last, rest, for one evening.

Morning courses through the slits in the curtains. Its light exposes the dust on the furniture. The dust in the air floats gently, unsettled in its directions and endeavors. His eyes gradually open, letting in trace amounts of light. He gets out of bed, shaking slightly from the coldness of his room. Like clockwork, he grabs his coat and cigarettes, walks out of his door, and makes his way to the shore where his boat rests anchored to a stack of rocks, his only solace.

The air is different, as if a storm is impending, he senses. Many years out on the ocean have taught him to detect the smallest changes in the air, anything that may affect the outcome of the catch.

Everything seems different.

It is not the ever-present layer of fog that descends upon Noumena during the fall, nor is it the gentle yet stinging rain that seems to fall out of the fog itself. A calm breeze makes it hard for him to light his cigarette. Stepping further through the fog down the muddy road introduces him to a headstone that he has previously not seen. Several weathered bricks and branches lay disheveled in a circle around it. It was as if it were covered in haste at the beginning, but the soul, in the end, rejected the idea of being hidden. The soul wanted witnesses to know who it was, but oddly, the name appears to be too deteriorated to pronounce. How lonesome it must be to only remain as a memory to another, sans the possibility to create anew.

The damp soil around the headstone begins to move in waves, synchronous to the rhythm of the ocean heard softly in the distance. Worms reach out of the roots and branches, eager to dance to the melody of melancholy, a catharsis of the past. It's time to go. He follows the echo of an angelic siren through the fog, that familiar calling of the ocean. He begins to disappear into the paleness of the surroundings, further and further to what he has known his whole life. The path seems longer today, perhaps because his watch stopped in the middle of the night. He will wait to see if his daily rhythm would be disrupted without his watch. Even though the end of the bottle marked the end of the night, those slow and steady hands helped to take the bottle out of his hands and guide him to bed. The fog becomes more dense with every step. The breeze gets cooler and stronger. The dirt road ends, leading to a vast shore of firm, grey sand that vanished. Seagulls, below a low ceiling of fog, drift slowly, precarious in their order and ventures. The stack of rocks by the pier anchors his boat. The ropes, fearless of battering winds and unforgiving storms. The rocks, steadfast in keeping the boat near the shore for its owner. He is there.

Chapter Four
Oceans

It is soothing to hear this gentle, repetitious sound. It has its own mind, its own purpose and reason for being. Like the Sirens, it draws the unsuspected to the shore, the cool water enveloping their feet, a wonder. It is calm. Nature's hypnotist. Memories are found here. The ones the heart allows to be found. It's easy to lose time here, the waves make sure of that. The clouds dwell above, looking down upon all, judging their motives, their souls with an equal eye. The birds are modern-day Valkyries, ready to take the willing to such great heights, incomprehensible to those below on the surface. Memories are made and memories are forgotten, but never relived. One can be alone here, and not feel the need for company. Its depth, like what's within, visible, but only at the surface. Sail across its glass surface, a mere reflection, two parallels. As unclear as the reflection may be, it's confounding when what we see is not what we want to see. Further within, darker, a space that light cannot reach or illuminate.

Chapter Five
Interlude

He feels that his wife is still with him, that they still are two as one. The ocean reunites them. He unties the ropes, pushes the boat out towards its center. The rain falls at a steady pace and the winds remain gentle. Grey clouds linger like a heavy-hearted man on past regrets and incidents. He stops the engine when the shore is no longer visible. It felt like hours, alone, physically, with the sounds of a natural world. No luck with the fish today. He lays down, the boat as a cradle, and gives his eyes a rest. Seagulls above send him delicate notes of a careless melody that eases his mind into a deep trance. Escape. Darkness. Time flies.

Chapter Six
Change

Sudden sounds. Open eyes. A seagull lies dead at his feet. His first deep breath at the sight chokes him. He immediately covers his nose and mouth with his jacket as the putrid stench relentlessly overwhelms his confused senses. Its wings have been brutally snapped in a horrific manner, with almost all of its feathers torn out to expose its leathery, lifeless patches of skin. He looks out across the ocean. He is alone, still. The waves are even calmer than how he remembered. If it is indeed a storm that is impending, it is not an ordinary one. The cloud cover remains right where it has been, as if the greatest artists of the world have painted his Heavens with the most realistic, depressing shades of grey in a magnificent still frame, worthy of being a memory. The rain falls lightly, as light as how it was before his sleep. What's missing? The wind, the seductive voice in his ears, and the hands through his hair. The ebb and flow of waves have calmed, and now are even quieter. He lifts the seagull with his feet and tosses it over, managing to make a splash that echoes all around him. The engine does not start. He begins to row his way back to shore. The fog gets thicker with every row of the paddle. He remains confident that his compass is still working. A dim light cuts a hole through the wall of white. It seems to be coming from the shore. A sense of anxiety sets in. He can't place his finger on what's causing the feeling. He recalls a familiar melody from his past to keep his nerves steady and focused. He rows faster. The dim light gets brighter until the light separates into two spherical orbs, side by side. The orchestra of seagulls have exited the stage, leaving only an open vacuum of silence for its audience. A faint hum can be heard in the distance, an eerie echo, one of an unfamiliar sound. The humming starts to work its way into his mind, his focus strays, his sight gets blurry. That dull, repetitious sound has irreversibly become the water, his paddle, his breath, his memory. His haven of solace has been breached, the Valkyries nowhere in sight. Row faster. Claustrophobia begins to set in. The fog is embracing, inches from his skin, a straitjacket of what was once his comfort. Shore is near. Every stroke of the paddle makes it harder to breathe. His compass has shattered from within. The two lights are now his compass. The directions are easy and clear. Primal. Get to the shore and destroy the lights. Destroy the source of the humming that overwhelms the familiar melody of his past. Do not let go of the past. Kill it. Kill anything that gets in the way. The sound, louder, the light, brighter. It is by the rocks where he anchors his boat. He steps onto shore and pulls his boat in. He grabs the ropes. Clockwork. He ties the boat down. He takes a paddle. The rocks haven't changed. They remain stagnant in stature, oblivious to the effects of the unnatural sound. How is it that the world around him is not affected by the unnatural, the unfamiliar? He thinks of how humans would react, taking such comfort in routine, the obvious. Anything unusual that isn't understood tends to be dismissed as foreign, strange, not normal. He feels trapped by his own biases. He falls into that category. His mind gets back on its feet, telling him to examine the unknown, louder and louder with each step through the damp sand. The fog hinders his movement, he cannot run for fear of what's beyond his senses, the constant drone, the distant lights. He has arrived at the center of his world. A car is in front of him.

How it got on shore without leaving a trail perplexes him. The doors are open, the engine remains running, and a thick branch is nestled between the seat and the steering wheel to keep the horn blaring. He stares, ruminating its purpose and why someone would lead him here. He snaps the branch out of place with his paddle. He then calmly ravages the car. Windows are shattered. Deep dents bruise the exterior. He smashes the headlights, patiently watching every piece of hot glass fall to the sand. It belongs there. The droning begins to distance itself from his mind. The lights leave his sight as his eyes brighten. Pieces of the broken paddle are scattered intricately around the car. He lights a cigarette. He breathes in the smoke of memory and breathes out the poison of memory. A defaced object rests before him. How did this get here? What happened to this car? Listlessly, he collects his composure, hums the tune of a familiar past, and walks towards a familiar dirt road. The fog clears, but the rain begins to fall harder. The features of the dirt road have blurred to look more like a smooth path into the unknown. What lies beyond the path, he is no longer sure of. What used to be a tranquil walk back home has become a journey of restlessness and unease. He slowly descends further into disquietude when he passes by the desecrated grave. He squints to keep the heavy raindrops out. His heart beats heavier and louder as he notices carvings of letters on the headstone that he couldn't see when walking by before. He backs away, eyes fixed on the illusion. Walk away, walk away, today has been strange, the hands of dawn have seized the day. It's surreal, no birds above, no rabbits to be seen or heard. The only sound being the lightness of rain, distant crashing of waves, his own footsteps, and heavy breathing. The road has ended, the one comfort he was able to perpetually rely on has fallen apart at his feet. He walks back to find the only other path to his house, one that leads through Noumena and a cemetery. He hasn't been down this path in years. He begins. The rain has stopped. Halfway down the path, an abrupt scream disturbs the silence, an echo of agony can be heard throughout the forest. It is loud, relentless, perpetual. A headache sets in and nausea takes over. The entire world is spinning to a different tune. His vision is blurry, off and on, as if staring within the snow on a television. An old record player begins to click and scratch a tune of familiarity, an invitation to dance and sway to the melody, a warm and lucid sound, beckoning him to dissolve into his background, to fade away and recollect the past, his wife, as if it's attempting to remind him that they are two as one. It is far way, but within his grasp, in the back of his mind. How could he ever forget?

Chapter Seven
Creature

From the shadows, a foul sight emerges, crawling ever so quietly out of the abyss. Feet by feet, row after row until it is close to being the length of his house. He is paralyzed, unable to comprehend what's slowly approaching him, eerily staring into his soul, starved to relish on his sins. Regain focus. The creature is like dew on a leaf, every detail is clear and picturesque, a grotesque sight to behold. Awe turns to fear as half of its body bends back and unfurls its arms to expose mangled limbs, bloody intestinal tracts, sheets of fresh skin, and row after row of human teeth all around a reflective object that shows him staring back at himself. The longer he stares, the faster time seems to fly. Its arms move rapidly in a hypnotizing manner and its orifices expand and contract to reveal blood-red eyes. Dinner for two. That sweet, sultry memory of romance overpowers the stench of burning flesh, decaying teeth, and decomposing matter that remains in the intestines. The record player is louder than he remembered. The sound of impending death bumps the needle out of place. The creature's mouth opens. Rolls of stitched flesh cascade to the ground without the help of gravity and multitudes of smaller mouths stem out like withered branches, sucking on the damp air and craving succulence of fear that drips out of his pores. The melody can no longer be heard. Primal. Destroy the source of the sound. Kill whatever is overpowering the melody. He unsheathes his hunting knife, all eight inches lightly rusted from the blood of countless fish. Its shine remained intact through years of use, but not for long. He pushes the blade downwards, incising raindrops until the tip penetrates the soft mouth on the stitched flesh and pins it to the soil. The instinct of survival has put him in a trance. He can no longer see his reflection. The mouth emits a dull tone of anguish. He refuses to hear its plea for release. The knife becomes a saw and severs the bloody mouth from the flesh. Severance of flesh, severance of self. Do not stop. He pierces the stitches, unraveling a variegated array of colors. Thick yellow bile, pulsating blue veins, sheets of red spraying blood, exposing its interior. He unstitches the rest of the flesh, dragging the blade downward to split the tongue into two thinner slabs of muscles and arteries in the darkest, most vile shade of red. Bloodlust. He then swings the knife towards its center, the mirror. A portion of the intestines is purged along with the scream from the creature's mouth. Blood spills to the ground from the gaping wound like ripe, aged wine poured from a cask into his mouth. Blood drunk. He repeatedly pierces its flesh, systematically spilling even more blood through fresh, stinging wounds. He rips off a sliver of flesh with the teeth attached. He grabs a limb that sticks out of its body and pulls it out immaculately. Before the creature can bellow out its rage, his hand enters its wound and blindly reaches his fingers out for an organ, a muscle, anything. A muscle beats at a steady pace. He wraps his hand around it and pulls it towards the light. The muscle tenses, disconnecting the arteries and veins, spreading the wound further apart as it exits the interior and becomes acquainted with an unfamiliar environment. The creature chokes on the sight of its inner organ, floating gently upon a thick puddle of blood. This is it, this is it. His knife enters its throat and he pulls down with such strength to split its body in two. Its insides are released. Beautiful organs flow freely amongst a waterfall of blood. The picturesque ground draws its body closer, to carry it back to where it came. Ashes to ashes. He backs away to allow Death to come apply the final brushstroke on this abstract painting of reality. Beautiful. Lifeless. Organs lay scattered. Their essence and purpose shutter with the cold palm of Death. Dust to dust.

His heavy breathing begins to get lighter as the wine wears off. His auditory nerves stretch their hands out to grasp on to whatever sound it can. The silence slips through his fingers, descending lighter than a feather from the most beautiful bird. The feather lands upon the instruments of Nature, its quills brushing up against the strings of tranquility. He falls to his knees and violently vomits at the heaps of flesh that remain, soon to be one with the Earth. This cannot be a dream, the feelings are too real. No words can truly describe his mind. The questions hide behind a thin veil of obscurity that has held reasoning as a prisoner, locked beyond the confines of his mind, further than his hands can reach. Skepticism floods the hallways of his veins, attempting to drown reality from within himself. The vulgar stench that leaves a wretched taste in his mouth is real. The thick blood that dries on his hands is real. The sound of the creature's twitching flesh is real. The reality in the mind is the reality of the world, with nothing to fill the space between. He remembers every detail of what has happened, every laceration upon its body, every emanation of fresh blood from its lesions, every inch of flesh disentangled by his knife. His reality is unraveling, the creature is penetrating his fortitude of sanity. Before its dead hands could wrap its fingers and clasp the sanity out of his mind, he gets on his feet and continues down the path towards Noumena.

Chapter Eight
Interlude

Humans are all vessels, emissaries of emotions and thoughts, gently drifting upon a river, guided by the currents of fate and choice, forever flowing blindly through dark forests amongst dim lighting towards similar ends and beginnings, never to look back upon the path from which they came.

Chapter Nine
Town

Reasoning returns and his head begins to clear. About a mile now for Noumena. Blood flow returns throughout his body, coloring over his pale frame with shades of tan. Regret. How can he regret? There is nothing to regret. It was survival. It was pure. Instinct. Primitive defense mechanisms. The rain falls continuously, a still frame from an old 8mm movie stuck on a loop. It is gentle enough to barely cause a stir amongst the puddles, to not disturb the natural aesthetic of stillness. The raindrops can't be seen, one would never notice it from inside, but it can be felt on the outside. It is cleansing, but only enough to wash away the simple things. Everything looks the same. He has been here, though he's never been here before. His inclinations guide his hands for a cigarette. Step by step, hastily, he progresses. The world is stagnant, unflinching towards the repeated tests of time. Darker and heavier the clouds become as he gets closer to Noumena.

The clock tower is visible beyond the tops of trees. It was originally intended to be a lighthouse, but somehow, ships would never be able to see the light, as if Noumena itself did not want to be seen. The light was then replaced by a mechanized clock, an artificial timekeeper, brought forth upon the town to count down the minutes of the day until nightfall when no one would notice time unfurling its wings and flying without the weight of humanity depending on its curse. He brushes his hand against the wall of the clock tower, searching to feel its age and to find the mouth that speaks of the history of the town. Nothing. Its mouth is sewn shut by the needle of neglect. Its age is purely skin deep, the exterior won't let him in any further. It itself is its own prison, a space where creation can become out of nothing, where memories are a corollary to the progression of time. His presence disrupts the tranquility of the still frame, shifting its powerful presence out of focus, no longer just a tower with recollections of the past, but now a sentinel of the present, brought to the light of the extant by his presence. His fingertips caress the prison, senses translucently passing through what remains of the past.

He reaches the outskirts of town. The town is drearier than he recalls. The walls of buildings are austere, the paint stripped to reveal its barren flesh, bleached yellow like the hands of skeletons in an open grave, reaching for grey skies and a pure rainfall. Nothing is pure here. The lights inside the buildings are dim, but enough to illuminate the emptiness that has swallowed the town whole. The decay wishes to tell the tale of the good and the bad, but not one person is around to listen. He glances through the foggy window of a derelict building. A dark yellow light bulb hangs from a string in the middle of the room, swaying like a recently used noose to the ebb and flow of a salty breeze that creeps ever so gently through the opening of the bleached window. The swaying of the light and his breathing are in tune, a perfect harmony amongst a sorrowful melody caressed by the ever-present bitterness of a desolate, melancholic reticence, well placed in his sullen heart of the matter. The windowpane does not reflect the world around him. His face, a silhouette, a caricature nestled within the perfectly shaped puzzle board of the surrounding backdrop. Flies lie on the floor beneath the bulb. Ineffable is the sight, such an allegory to aspirations, as the flies lie listlessly on the earth from which they have arisen, on a natural path of migration towards the light, towards a higher state and self. Every path has an end in this existence. Such an intimate betrayal it is when the end becomes entwined with the present, so sincere, innocent, and expected. Transcendent is the light and the absence of light within and without the end. Shells that compressed an entire life span of a being within the anatomical, biological, and physiological threads of physicality and reality released from this existence at the speed and continuity of time linger on the ground as relics beneath the bulb. The light, faintly out of reach, as faint and fine as the sands of the beach, as infinite and cosmic as the skies above and the oceans below. He turns away, ephemerally gazing at the town before him. Memories were made here. History remains here. History must have buried the memories within the walls of these buildings. The echoes of their voices can be heard through its enclave, prisoners of their own creation. Their lips have fallen silent for some time.

A distant melody catches him unsuspectedly, delving deep into his well of memories, lifting his body into a trance, idly guiding him towards a derelict building on the edge of town. As the melody gets louder, the more vivid and corporeal his memories become. The cold bricks of the building begin to crumble to make way for the warm walls of his home. Come close. The rusted wooden planks that lay before his feet regain color, becoming an inviting porch with two rocking chairs. Almost here. The darkness inside the room is illuminated, gently tucking away years of darkness into circular corners. The emptiness is replaced with a dining room table and an old record player. A romantic dinner for two. The smell of rust and decay become ambrosial, shifting in airiness until his senses are stimulated with crisp notes of tender rain showers in early spring. The melody has taken him back. He steps onto his porch. The chairs gently sway back and forth to the rhythm of sweet memories. He turns around to look back upon Noumena. It has become the sunset he has always remembered and can never forget. The disproportionate, abandoned relics of bygone days are replaced with the sanguine strength of green trees and lustrous hills. He steps through the door, dubiously treading upon the comforting flooring towards the dining room. The sounds of shattered glass whirling across the flowing wooden surface cannot be heard. The floors cordially welcome his footsteps, cradling his feet with consummate placidity and guiding the limbs farther into the embrace of a tender painting elucidating a loving home. The portrait is perfect, a masterpiece. He hears a mellow hum that can barely be caught over the record, as if it wishes to not be revealed. The delicate redolence of the ocean caresses his rough skin with a soothing touch, filling his body with yearning and consolation. He senses a presence around him, close enough to make his heart beat faster, yet too far to know what it is. His memory, his heart beckons him to remember who or what it may be. He feels doubtful, as if he knows this is a dream. Before closing his eyes and falling into the pool of repressed memories, he hears the lightest of footsteps, so quiet and innocent that anybody else would be bemused of hearing anything. The walls unfold its hands to ethereally impel him towards the bedroom. Time ceases, it seems. His hand steadily shakes as it nears the door handle. The melody of the record wraps its fingers around his, entwined forwards and towards. The dulcet scent of cherry blossoms surrounds his senses, trapping them under its spell of pure felicity. No escape from the beauty of naturality. Who could escape? Who would want to escape? The door opens. He stands struck in motionlessness as the flood overtakes his thoughts.

It's as if he were dreaming.

Chapter Ten
Interlude

Blinding is the light that illuminates the darkest and most repressed of memories, so overwhelming is the view of what was that that itself is the illusion that makes the mind wander from what it truly was that led the mind there to begin with.

Chapter Eleven
Traverse

An allusion to the past has been made, a connection, no matter the strength of the signal, established and embedded into the current, forever to be an imprint, the lighthouse that illuminates only so far out beyond an ocean of restricted time and hazy recollections. The voyage lasts a lifetime, with the past reminisced, the present lived, and the future dreamed. The ocean is the map, the waves guiding the ship towards where it is meant to go at this time or in time. The currents, no matter how treacherous or deceiving, remain by the ship at all times, guardians of the vessel, never letting loose of the keel of the ship, its grip as sure as the embrace of gravity upon the bodies of men. The ship stops at numerous islands, representations of choices to be made, alternate tangents that the voyage could follow. Which tangent to be followed though, depends on the captain, the individual. Each ship, on its maiden voyage, concurrent to the cadence of the apex of waves that breathe ever so freely across the surface of this Earth. May the moon become the compass, may the heart gravitate towards its desires and wishes, may dreams be the reason of reality being so.

Memories are sullen, yet they are beautiful, becoming more precious as time passes. Memories are gifts given from the present to the past, wrapped in elegance with the ribbons of every hour, every day that passed and continues to. An entire life passed, compressed within and scattered throughout the space of mind, the joyous events, childhood, the melancholic moments, death of loved ones, brought to the light of anamnesis as desired.

The scent of salt, sweet and tranquil, never acutely piercing, but salient enough to awaken and revive docile senses. As the body and the vessel become one, every motion of the wave, from the crest to the base, pacifies and soothes the darkest of thoughts and recollections. Means of reconciliation become illuminated and the self can peer within the mirror that has long stood before him. The reflection, as deluding as thieves and traitors, to those unwilling to confront what lies beneath.

The ocean, as expansive as the fields of Elysium, as far as the eyes are allowed to see, in pure harmony with the skies above. The space between the perfectly formed clouds and the cool mist that splashes out of the darkness of the swirling waves is the domain where time thrives. Time flies, its wings manmade with the nails of perpetuity and the steel of requisiteness.

He falls, supine position, into the ocean, let loose from the grip of the vulture of time. It hovers above him, circling in rhythm, waiting for his body to rise to the surface. His body sinks, deeper and deeper into a realm where time is no longer the judge, the immortal, the infinite, that it is above the surface. It is ethereal, peaceful, lonesome. The only presence felt is from the warmth of fond memories of seasons past. The depth of the ocean is a cradle, its coolness and the heat of his body now singular. Its arms forever open, as loving as a mother embracing her child, no matter the time past, no matter the distance between. The entrancing chant of waves crashing upon the rocks of solidarity beg those in passing to come closer, to relinquish the bruising grasp on the hands of eternity.

The darkness of the unknown becomes the perfect backdrop, the perfect allusion and illusion, a mirror to the opposites and its balance in this existence. The absence of, or the antithesis of what is known, acknowledged, and remembered, follows the body to the bottom of the ocean, with each shortened breath underwater strengthening the unknown, where memories collide, a beautiful field of chaos just before physical death. This is where shapes melt, losing edges and dimensions, as the palette of colors that adorned the warmest and most loving of memories become consumed by the salt of the ocean, the propagation of the unknown. Disconnected patches of skies, heavy clouds that vary in shades of grey, the scent and taste of salt from the ocean. Such beauty that is forgotten when time is the judge, dictator, and creator of how one lives out their life. Let the monetary, the physical, have the highest of values. Nature will always survive in the end, no matter the length of lives.

Humanity will be extinct before Nature fades, but, as dictated by time, human nature will value Nature and the Earth as second to physical possessions and the pecuniary. Time is not to be embodied by the minutes and seconds that pass unwaveringly from the ends of the oscillating pendulum, but to be crystalline, unwithered against the momentum and forces of mankind, its axiom as precious as the most coveted diamond.

Close your eyes and let the currents take you where they may. We are merely in passing.

Chapter Twelve
Path

Resurface from reliving repression. He stares blankly into an empty room. He quickly turns around in attempt to retrieve the fleeting melody of the record player. It's gone. Gone from his senses, but not from the back of his mind. The walls revert back to their disparaging selves, the floorboards lose their ornate, natural color, fading into a thick layer of dust. Just another building suffering from physical and temporal abandonment. His eyes fall to the ground to see that there are only footsteps below him, not anywhere else in the building. The dust parts with every step he takes towards the front door. There is no sunset. Just another grey sketch of the sky with faint vertical lines of rain spaced evenly amongst the picturesque ambience. He steps onto mud that smothers the Earth and surrounds every aberrant structure. This town used to impress itself upon him, but now it is merely an intentional fallacy. His heart is heavy, but he won't let it touch the ground that will one day consume him with its stimulating, frail hands, to become a fragment of someone's recollection, someone's past, when his physical self is no longer present, but in its grasp. His footsteps are delicate, they press down on the mud and its hands press up on his feet. So light and fragile are his imprints that he does not leave a trail, a ghost, wandering capriciously to and from obscure destinations. His soul remains systematic and perpetual. The structures stand firm, emanating a stillness that has attenuated the intuition of ataraxia, defiant to all lost cause and fabricated hope. The castles in the air have crumbled. Everyone knew of it. The affinity that had been imbued within those that needed it most had been secularized. Everyone felt it. The remnants hailed down upon them, absorbed through even the most ardent of coating, a downpour of corporeal punishment and spiritual absolution. This is the purveyor of eschatology at its darkest. The pillars of the ruins that once bolstered glimmering reveries have receded in unison with the ebb and flow of the incessant ocean tides that ride amongst the winds of dilapidation. Incessancy is not certain, nor ordained, thus the comfort of a constant is demarcated to one's perspicacity. A mile into the future is not the same as the mile in the past. The process of recollection does not abide to the framework of time. The salt of the ocean will be spread over the graves of Noumena. Nature will reclaim what rightfully belongs to it.

Come what may. Let perpetuality narrow the pathway on which humanity walks upon. Eyes are sewn shut, the blood from the pricks of punctures have dried, a sign of permanence of continuity and an insignia of what has been. Bodies are emaciated, longing for a nurturing sense of comfort that has long been buried below before blighted eyes of the sky, amongst the fertile, vitriolic ground, the eventual resting place.

Sweeping hills
of weeping willows,
weeping widows
reap, sow, repeat.

Cries above
and rain below,
all ties severed,
Nature revered.

Sunrise
and sunset,
meager lives
merely bereft.

Phoenix wings
extend upward,
sins of mankind
spiral downward.

Lessons unlearned,
as cities burn,
beneath the ground,
we witness rebirth.

As he ponders the path before him, for reasons unknown, he
recollects upon a specific moment. His neighbor, a fellow
fisherman, out on the ocean in a sudden, treacherous storm,
many years ago when they were amateur navigators of the blue
fields. So close to death, so close to the end, yet they had
survived. Reasons upon reasons disputed, as to how they made it
back to land, but both knew that their questions for each other
and the answers sought were not in regards to how, but why they
lived that day. Perched on a cliff near the wreckage of their boat,
their lives and their faith were questioned, and whether it was
strengthened or weakened, could have only been seen within the
actions they would choose to make throughout their remaining
days. Mark Vice, his name was, a name that's as clear as the
skies past. A maverick of the tides, a seneschal of his own fate.
An autonomous ruler of his vessel, perceptible and intangible. It
eased his mind, he used to say, being alone amongst the field of
Nature's sinuous hair. The buoyancy of his body pressed freely
upon the ebb and flow of what's below, his boat, a mere cradle,
a syncopation of utmost tranquility and resilience, where
allusions and dreams coalesce. The wreckage changed Mark, as
if his outstretched hands touched an elusive physicality of the
unknown. Amidst the tempting currents, amongst the liquid
fields, he was always searching, hands oscillating in darkness,
longing for the touch once more. He never knew what he was
searching for, but recurrently connoted how there was something
out there, on the water, below the drift, waiting to be unveiled
and understood. The pursuit became an obsession, breathing
affirmation into his life. The writing is on the wall.

Chapter Thirteen
Empty-handed

Two as one. We are but two entities at a harmonious balance. How tragic that we are always searching for the other being, yet it does not exist in this space. There's a feeling, an allure from the ocean herself, sprinkled ever so delicately upon the wisps of salt that leave the currents, abstrusely laced through the masterful symphony that the waves compose upon terra firma. The land is but a theater, where we are the curious gathering awaiting a reprieval amidst a reprise, the condemnation of the material for a sense of longing of what is intended and natural. The chains of a materialistic world clamp stringently around our limbs, mankind's bond forged forcibly stronger with every innovation and lustful subjugation of what was once thought unconquerable. The tides will rise as the conductor begins to orchestrate and guide its musicians. A weaving harmony pierces the skin as lamentation draws eyes downwards, within. The salt of the ocean will cleanse all wounds, medicated, as we all are. The vitriolic wine, the drunken revelry, the dance of intangibility, the traits that make mankind manmade marionettes, modeled and molded by us, to be manipulated by manmade machines, the bane and crutch of the existence of humankind. The dissonance is deafening, but only momentarily, until paralysis sets in, with only the eyes to look to the skies to shiver in sheer solitude, forever mournful over how blind our race has been. Will anything ever change? It will never change. The calm, the resilience, elusive as the concepts that attempt to explain such perceptions, lost to the endless abyss ahead and below. The skies offer remorse, yet the depths of the water refrain from affection, choosing to only provide a cradle to those that venture across her surface. Look beyond, look through the darkest depths, to see that one is merely looking within. What is it that we are searching for? What is it that we are running from? Mirrors can only show so much of what we want to see. Look through, look beyond to see what cannot be unseen.

Chapter Fourteen
Plagues

The ocean holds the answers, the depths are the levels, we are the monsters, amongst Gods and Devils.

Chapter Fifteen
Walk

Mark. Where has he gone? Has he fallen victim to desolation along with Noumena? The uncertainty weighs heavily on his consciousness, pressing down on his reasoning and curiosity until his feet gain traction on the surface beneath and perpetuates progressive physical movement towards a destination that retains a dense haze upon an unclear, winding path. He sets out for the answer, but must make haste, for a skulking sense of loneliness lives in the shadow of his body, a foreboding sentiment of a world closing in on him, where the voices in his mind and the architects of the past attain malicious intentions of lacerating the physical self, as if the shadow were an anchor pulling him under, away from progress and hope. He is alone. He urges his thoughts to focus on the task at hand, but the shadow never leaves, fixated on bringing out the worst from within the somber recesses of his mind. Despite the forlornness, he remains resolute, and with that in mind, he continues onwards. Further down, he sees a house, and though it takes the shape and color of any of the other residences around Noumena, he feels a slight optimism that that is Mark's house. His footsteps, desperate and worrisome, hasten to get to the house, to break the spell of loneliness, to be around the company of another physical being once again. Unfamiliar, physically, as the house may seem, he steps up to the porch, his feet as hesitant as his hand before knocking on the front door. Mark opens the door, inviting him in without a word, as if he were expecting him. They make their way to the living room, an inviting atmosphere with a glowing fireplace to battle the frigid outside temperatures, and occupy seats opposite of each other. Concentrate.

Chapter Sixteen
Discourse

"I'm glad you've made it, I've been waiting for quite some time. This weather's only getting worse. Not what I'm used to."

"Mark, I'm surprised you're still here, I can't seem to find anyone else around town, it's like they just disappeared."

"It's different though, lately the ocean, she's becoming more of a home than what I'm standing in now. It's the weather, I know it is."

"I'm not quite sure what it is you're trying to say, I can barely recall our time out on the waters, I don't even know why I'm here, the path just led me here. Whatever is happening though, it's changing everything about what I remember."

"You make it sound like it's a burden to bear, but it's not. It's beautiful, but poisonous to easily recall what's gone, in the exact way you want it to be, to freeze it in some form of isolated suspension, where it's as one-sided as your own variation of your perceived reality. I hope I'm making sense. I hope you recognize your blatant ignorance, because it's as far from bliss as your reality."

"What are you trying to imply? My memories are tainted by my biases? That I'm selective over what I choose to remember and how I remember them? It's a part of my past, not anyone else's."

"You're right, I am sorry about my mannerisms, and for delving into an obviously sensitive subject. I'm usually not as giddy or excited about having company over, but this is truly a special, memorable, and of course, expected occasion. We don't have to celebrate, but I'm going to have a drink, or two, or however many it takes to allow me to speak my mind. What's your poison for this moment? Wait, let me guess, whiskey, foreign, aged at least thirty years. I know you pretty well, along with your vices."

"We haven't seen each other or spoken in years, but you're right, you do know me very well, I'll have one drink, thank you."

"One for now, it'll be. Now tell me, what brought you here, to the edge of the world, at the end of the world? Are you here to repent? To gain a sliver of redemption in the tumultuous life you've lived so far?"

"I don't understand what you're asking, and what do you mean by the end of the world?"

"Surely you've witnessed what's transpired, what changes you've brought upon Noumena. Whether you're aware of being the harbinger or not though is a completely different conversation."

"You've seen it as well, what's been happening? What is going on? Why all of a sudden is everything changing?"

"As much as I can tell, it seems that you're ready for the next step, it's fabricated and elevated for you, and all you have to do is reach out for it. You've done well so far, exactly what was intended for someone like you. It's good to recognize your ignorance before this life is over. How do you feel? Are you comfortable?"

"I don't know what to do, you're asking questions that I don't have answers to, I don't know where I'm headed."

"We are all an embodiment, the creator and the destroyer, of the physical and the nonphysical. You're so complacent with where you were, but I see now that you're changing. And with such change comes a vast division in physicality from what was and what will be."

"How are you a part of this change? If what you're saying is true, then you are also able to create and destroy what's around us and what's within you. How is it that the world is only changing for me? You don't seem at all affected by these sudden changes. Unless you and I share the same view of what is happening, where we beget a blueprint of what's happened and a timeline of what will materialize, but that's a fallacy, the two of us can't occupy concurrent planes of existence. The only way that would be feasible is if you and I are the same, where we are a duality in one form."

"Is that scenario as preposterous as it sounds? Is that a possibility? With everything that has occurred and is occurring, I feel that anything is plausible. Nothing is as it seems lately, wouldn't you agree? But you, James, you're afraid of the unknown, despite knowing that you are the creator of your own destiny. Will you choose to be the savior of this manifested world or merely play the role of a test subject, a marionette suspended from the strings of fate's hands?"

"I do, and I am, but why am I here? There has to be a reason why I've arrived at this place, at this time. I could've blindly followed the masses and its supposed trajectory, at least I would've known where it would've led me, therefore having more answers than I have now, along with an alluring sense of calm."

"But to stray and wander is to open your eyes. Wouldn't you agree? You came for answers to questions that you don't know how to ask, and where to begin with these questions? Well, quite simply, it's already begun. You see, self-discovery and self-refutation are the finest, purest ways of obtaining answers. Simply being given an answer touches the surface of the motive, pure memory. No work involved, no soul seeking. We branch out for support or motivation, when what we seek is already within us. We need to reach in to form the answers with our own hands in an effort to take hold of it and pull it to the light. To create, from within, and destroy what unsettling troubles we may have in this physical realm. The power to create and destroy, a uniquely human trait, singular and collective. In physicality, we can create and destroy an object's physical form. It may no longer exist, but it does leave traces of its existence. These traces become a physical form as well, like a memory or a bad dream, where it never truly is destroyed. Destruction is more complex than creation. One must erase all associations with that object, the labels and the reasoning behind each label. But in the midst of such process, one must lose their way, erase the process of getting to the reasoning for having labels. It's practically impossible while you're still human though, our subconscious is notorious for piecing together and bridging gaps between vacant spaces with implausibility, coincidence, and fragments of fate and choice. 'Cogito ergo sum.' On the other hand, to truly create requires communication between language and rhetoric, the ability to identify and label. Labeling is the goal of letters where symbols and sounds converge. When we see an object, consciously or in our subconscious, we immediately take notice of its physical aspects, size, shape, color, textures, and the like. We then formulate, based on those aspects observed and learned, its purpose and reason for being. But, what's formulated varies between individuals, as our comprehension and the meaning we attach to the object can differ to such an extent that the one object itself can become indistinguishable from its own reflection. Therefore, an assumption can be made that we as humans only get out of something what we put into it."

"Language is the virus, memory is the disease, choice is the culprit, and fate is the fallacy."

"You're expanding, your mind is wandering now, your apprehension is pushing beyond the ends of the horizon. You see, within us is a chaotic realm, a vast, infinite space without any boundaries. Within such realm is where we create the world we live in. But once it is created, established, manifested, we fall into a comfortable state where we only expand our universe in small increments. Within one's lifetime, this mental prison can widen by leaps and bounds or reverse and grow smaller, confining us within a cell of singularity, where the physical, material world becomes our obsession. This mental prison is fluid, varying in size and thickness of bars, based on what we perceive to be important. Some bars are transparent, but are still there. You haven't opened your mind, expanded your prison. You've focused solely on your career, your wife, for so long and with such admirable intention that your only escape from your self-imposed prison will be in death. But it wasn't your death that affected the boundaries of your prison. It was the death of your wife. Such a tragic event should've pushed your boundaries farther out, but it seems to have had an adverse effect and made it smaller to where your mind set its own limitations on what to think, what to remember, what to feel, what to forget."

"First of all, she's not dead, I know she isn't, I can sense it."

"And off we begin on the course of a new tangent. I believe you, trust me, and I sincerely hope you do find her. In regards to death, it's not what you fear. Death itself is a transformation, from one state to another, not always in a physical manner. Even beyond death, we still remain in place, remnants lost in reverie amongst blurry photos of infinity and eternity. You had an awakening. In the darkest realms of your mind, you would've perpetually decayed in your own volitional misery. We all have our awakenings. Every choice we make has the chance of being an awakening. Once the choice is made, all we can do is press onwards, oblivious that that choice itself is a provocation of one's own. And remember, pondering the path of the choice that wasn't made is a mere speculation as to what may have happened, a world unto itself."

"So what is choice? Is it a power given to every rational being that thinks in the effort to retain a sense of control, power, and order amidst a chaotic universe? Sure, the realm outside of our mind is chaotic, but what we hold within is far more disorderly, a morbidly beautiful cacophony of disarray, a never-ending staircase that spirals within the panopticon of mental chaos and laconic unison. Choice must be a wormhole, a portal of sorts, where what we think, the images we see in our minds, the unbecoming of imagination, the creation of dreams, the depthless ocean of emotions that binds us to existence, converge in harmony with the realm of physicality, materiality, tangibility, and the five basic human senses. Through this wormhole, we are allowed to travel back and forth simultaneously, to entwine both the world within us and the world outside of us in such a manner that they overlap and amalgamate."

"Thus, the result is what we would call existence. Choice may sometimes feel like fate when, for example, things fall together in such a sporadic order that there's no other way of explaining or reasoning with the outcome. Perhaps it's simply luck. Even when things fall apart, they have to fall somewhere, and we hope that the pieces of the event that had caused the dissolution fall back into place in a manner where the outcome becomes better than what it previously was, or at least back to the original state that it was in. This leads us to fate. There is always that lingering fear within us that we have no control over anything that happens. We may mistake choice as fate, and fate as choice, depending on one's outlook. If fate is the dominant force that rules our entirety of existence, what do we live for? Unless each choice we make branches off from the tree of life into a separate tangent, each with its own predetermined ending and finale on this stage of life. Absolutes are fate. Death is absolute, the road to Death, regardless of which path one takes, is absolute. What comes after, we'll never know until we're there. Imagine this analogy as a symbolism of living and dying."

"We are all on a train. We are all unaware of how we got on, and there appear to be no stops along the way. Constant, perpetual motion. Without worrying or thinking about how we got here to begin with, we immediately begin to stare out of the window at the wonders that we're seeing. We see things that are beautiful, comforting, unique, like the ocean and the changing of the seasons. We also see things that leave us somber, reflective, depressed, like graveyards and desolation. The train ride lasts for what feels like an eternity in our minds and perspectives, but the train itself is perpetual and rhythmic to the ticking of the clock. We see things in the distance, eagerly anticipating the magnitude of its beauty, yet they remain blurry and mysterious. It feels like forever while we're waiting to see the future and what's coming up, but when we finally do see it, we forget about the time that we've spent simply waiting for it. Afterwards, we look back on the path we've been on and realize how far we've come, and though the train is still at a steady pace, we feel that we've gone so far. Objects and events witnessed in the past start to fade into the background of melancholy, regrets, and memories. Eventually, we enter a dark tunnel. Time becomes artificial and the train moves at different speeds for everyone. Without knowing what's outside in the darkness or what's coming soon, we cling to the memories we have and the time we have remaining. Then there's a light in the distance. We stare, awestruck as to what it could be, what we will see next. The light blinds us. We close our eyes and everything disappears."

"I would like to believe that we end up at an interchange station, awaiting a transfer, suspended in a trance, eager to know what it is that we are expecting, curious as to why we are there, reminiscing over a past that doesn't exist in that dimension. Then a train arrives, offering different things to see and experience, and thus we embark on our new journey. Should that happen, I would not know that it's another train, but simply a train. Who knows, it could've been my first, twentieth, or final ride, but at that time of knowing, all I would know is that it's my one and only. There is a continuum, a loop that we're all in, like atoms and molecules, all floating through a vast vacuum of inanition. We are our own solar system, galaxy, and universe. Never close to anyone or anything, but all moving on a specific trajectory. Two worlds within us, soul and mind, the physical and the spiritual, material and intangible, both separate but equal, two as one. What are we? What are we meant to be? What are we destined for? What quietly awaits us at the terminus? Sift through the falling autumn leaves and traverse the fog lingering in the graveyard. Look below. Look within and close your eyes. Let that feeling of confinement, that feeling of dwelling in your mind's prison guide you towards becoming and unbecoming. Let knowledge be the hands that create order in chaos. Order only creates a circle of light around us. Its rays can only reach certain depths in certain places. Sometimes, this is what we settle for. The light illuminates and enlightens us. We are here and we want people to know that we exist, whether it may be through a faint, fragmented memory or a strong, telling connection, we wish for others to acknowledge our permanence."

"If that's the case, then we are alive to some, and dead to others. The memory of a person dictates whether we exist to them or not. Our light, our existence, can only shine so far, like the beacon of a lighthouse. The extent of our light can fade or become brighter in time and no matter how dim the light can get, so long as the memory exists, the light is there, we ourselves just can't see how bright."

"Well said. Constant perpetuality within our minds negates the stagnation we feel in this physical world. Our memories are reels of moving images recorded in the past, always on a loop, like a record, with a beginning, middle, and end. The longing for the past, as fleeting and deceptive as it may be, fades a little further into obscurity as time passes, but never too far, as if our longings are on an orbit, pulled closer and pushed further, by gravity, circling around the very core of our universe, our existence. Everything correlates, everything is within and around us. Connection between humans, and the building and maintaining of it, is absolutely necessary and vital, yet tragic and short-lived."

"How lonely it must be to be the only one living."

"Uncomfortably lonely, trust me, I would know. It's a burden that weighs heavier than anything in this world, the human condition, the union and companionship that we all seek to find and keep. Humans are a fallible affliction, resorting to measures that meddle in the thresholds of dreams and nightmares, so long as the connection is established. The reality is that dreams and nightmares are portals or wormholes down a rabbit hole of unknowing, a world where our physical world materializes amongst the fields of an alternate reality. Remember what I said about two seemingly distant ideas or objects converging as one state of being? Same theory applies. The possible and the impossible, the fiction and the non, the ethereal and the material collide together in such a manner and orderly succession that science, math, and music, the arts of the universe, become stripped of its absolutes, creating a new, separate void of being, where our mind's eye is virginal and open to new levels of consciousness, lying in transit from one's consciousness down to the subconsciousness, and ultimately, the unconsciousness. This is a dimension where gravity and physics are defied, monuments and towers change in physicality, ordinary humans become savage animals, and anything else that we deem to be impossible while we are not within them. Contrary to this idea that the mass of men may believe to be true, our dreams, our nightmares, are interconnected to our realities. They cross the threshold of our peripheral boundary of what is possible, creating parallels, or like a bridge to nowhere, though you are aware of where this bridge will lead to. This world is not unordinary, nor is it to be taken lightly and brushed off to be permanently forgotten and uncommitted to memory. Our reality is a reflection of dreams, like a man peering within a puddle of water. The man can see his reflection in the murky water, but is not aware of what may be beneath. If this is the case, then there are numerous worlds within and around us. It just seems that we have become comfortable in 'this' physical and material world, as if we are not aware that such comfort, stagnation, or entropy simply makes the bars of our mind's prison thicker, harder, and colder. Through dreams and nightmares, our consciousness slips through the bars of our prisons and experiments and flirts with the darkness on the other side of our darkness."

"Does everything in this world have to hold meaning or a reason for being? Who are we to decide what exists or not? I can't tell whether I'm dreaming or awake anymore. Everything right now feels ethereal, surreal, even mesmerizing. It feels like my dreams and nightmares are creeping into my conscious state, slowly replacing what I find to be normal and usual. Everything that I've found comfort in, the familiarity of what's around me, has disappeared. Something happened when I was out on the ocean and fell asleep, maybe this is what happens when time no longer exists. I feel like I'm sleepwalking, but I know what I'm doing in that specific moment, at that exact time without having to recollect. I feel like I'm spinning, floating through this world, but something is holding my hand, guiding me. The only piece of certainty, the imperium, the absolute, that I possess is the record player. That's the only thing I understand and care for. It's on a continuous loop in my head and I know the reason why."

"That sensation, that feeling, is completeness, you're in between the bars of your prison, you're almost out into the unknown. But to go further, you must revert. The record player is the anchor that chains you within your prison. Without that anchor, you will be free to escape your prison here on this plane of existence. You're not quite living, and you're not quite dead, you're stepping out of what you deem to be comfortable, the familiar, this material world, into the unknown, the world you've been flirting with within your dreams and nightmares, a higher level of being, a more expansive, deeper level of consciousness. You're no longer bound to your prison, this is your chance to escape, now that you know how. You are the creator and the destroyer. So be still, let your mortal coil unravel. Loosen the anchor and drift apart from yourself, let go of everything you know right now."

"The record player? The melody? You're telling me that I should let go of my most precious memory, to do what? Become a martyr? A God? Am I in limbo?"

"Depends on what you choose to believe. To some, this is Hell, and to others, Heaven, a harmonic balance of neutrality in this chaotic plane of existence. You can call me the gatekeeper, and if you'd wish, I could guide you to a higher level of euphoria or I can guide you down the path to misery and a hellish existence."

"So am I dead?

"How else would you have made it here?"

"I honestly don't know. This all simply feels like a continuation of what I last remember. I went out on my boat. I fell asleep. I woke up and..."

"...everything had changed."

"The only certainty that I know and possess is the image..."

"...and sound of the record player."

"The melody..."

"…is cascading, transcending."

"It overshadows and encompasses everything."

"It's as if…"

"…I'm dreaming."

Chapter Seventeen
Marionette

What a lovely reflection of what has transpired. His eyes open, the layers of light slowly filtering through the curtains bring his sight to the present moment. The dust exposes the age of his neighbor's house as it gently settles on any object that stands still. His neighbor, where did he go? All that remains in Mark's place is an eloquent Victorian-era mirror that somehow hasn't collected any dust. He must've been speaking to himself, a ghost. How lonely it must be to be the only one living. He finishes his drink, glances at the bottle on the table, but remains tenacious and abstains from the temptation. It is time to move on. He rises to his feet and notices a thin layer of dust on his clothing. How long has he been resting and ruminating?

With all that is known as a probable fallacy in logic and reasoning, he is at a standstill, with nowhere to turn but the supposed trajectory that he has followed thus far. The ocean, her allure, his solace, there is no other path. The sirens of a reality unrealized, the singularity that emanated from the duality within the self, led him to an expeditious, caustic realization that the said path has been paved in gold this whole time, amicable and pernicious, delicately awaiting and embracing his steps along the way.

Chapter Eighteen
Atonement, or the Obscuration of Despondency

Recognize your ignorance, prepare your obituary, let the eulogy of those left in your wake guide you to the Isles of the Blessed, for you carry the burden of disseminating the dissolution of your humanity from the ashen fingertips of the incisive machine of perpetuality and forthright semblance.

Chapter Nineteen
Palettes of Light and Dark

His body stirs the staleness lurking in the air as he steps outside. Nothing has changed. Was anything supposed to? The dialogue exchanged felt as if it were a script, every theme predestined to be discussed, every question and accompanied answer left to the individual's mind for translation to enlightenment. Where is the light in enlightenment? A dark matter indoctrinated to shy away from the light of optimism, the absence of color in the life of the martyr, by the metallic machine of burden that anchors all of mankind to the most prominent and inevitable of emotions, while the undercurrents of nescience flow freely upon the tranquil river of time towards an ocean of stolidity. This dialogue then was not merely preordained, but prewritten. It had to lead to this, a brief moment in time, a small ripple in the river. Unexpected, was his arrival. Expected, was his presence. Unexpected, were the questions. Expected, are his next steps. Every move now is no longer guided by the soft left hand of salvation and the scaly right hand of fate. Without a physical destination in the realm of this current reality in mind, he knows where he must end.

Is there such path as one of righteousness? If it is to be believed, then the errors of humans are merely glitches and blips in the signals of the machine. The path that most people take is illuminated by preconceptions and hope, and to some, religion, never revealing much of what may come, but always showing enough to keep us on the path. To stray is to go an unknown way, where the decisions made at each opportunity throughout existence alters the ground on which our feet will land. Nothing is certain, though going against the grain and proposing one's own path can lead to less pain when realization is at the end of the line.

He makes his first choice, both monumental and feeble, with clarity and doubt. Making his way down the hill, the sounds of a painful existence begin to weave discreetly into his vision of reality. This is the pain that comes with time, linear and singular. His path through this darkened world is illuminated. This is a new frontier, one that shifts shapes, colors, and dimensions. Temporal and corporeal movements are unhinged from the hooks that used to suspend him over a shared vision of an esoteric sense of omnicompetence that the masses have succumbed to. Time loses its importance. Time is merely linearity, progression, but only in the sense that it moves forward at the constancy and perpetuality of the heart that beats within his chest. This is the relinquishment of reality at its purest.

Chapter Twenty
Watch and Listen

His eyes make way to the object around his wrist. A leather band with a square piece of silver metal, held together by a clasp. The face of the object is blank. Ashes rest within the face, aimlessly swaying like waves with the movement of his arm. Look closer. Imprints encircle the inner square, markers of some sort. An artifact, a fossil, a relic from another time. What is it? A sense of reasoning and recollection flee from his mind, despite efforts of attempting to remember. He feels that there is a reason why the object is on his wrist, as if it was of utmost importance and relevance at one point in time. He leaves it on, believing that in time, he will recognize the reason for its being.

Chapter Twenty-One
Wandering

She is with him. No matter how dim or bright, she is the only light.

Chapter Twenty-Two
The Painter

The skies remain unfocused, blurry as the depth of the puddles that he walks by. Shades of grey create keen outlines and vivid layers above him, a mural of aural beauty within the painting of this landscape. The notion of perpetuality is exemplified as he makes his way through a forest of bamboo. Every step he takes becomes an addition to the painting. The brushstroke of the painter changes to illustrate and illuminate the finest details of the forest. Audial tranquility and the gentle kiss of falling mist upon his skin adds a touch of docile color to his perception. It is calming here within the embrace of the verdant pillars of Nature. It is a stark contrast between what is above and what is around him. Beauty is not defined by means of physicality, but by the esoteric state of being that it instills when in its presence. Further in, the trees meld closer to one another, as if to block his way. Claustrophobia descends, aiding the motives of the trees. Eyes dilate. Trees grow taller. Contemplation of moving forward settles in, raising questions as to why he keeps walking in the direction that he is. There must be a reason. There is. He struggles to make his way through the narrow path between the trees, careful not to disrupt the elegance and fragileness of Nature. What lies ahead? Ahead, a clearing. Shades of vibrant green, in front and beyond, determine the distance between. Closer and closer, pushing through, further and farther. The clearing gets brighter to reveal a field of systematically placed rocks that resemble the ebb and flow of waves. At last, he steps foot on the arrangement, careful as to not disrupt its ornate nature of idleness. The rocks are visually stimulating, a discrete, harmonious relation between objects of Nature. A serene, meditative breeze of rest and peace caresses his body. His eyes close and lungs expand to allow all the tranquility that he may inhale.

Here, the balance between man and Nature is at its most pure. This is where the balance should be. For so long, mankind has tipped the scale of existence towards the advancement and empowerment of itself, while Nature and naturality has been chained to hindsight and ignorance.

As if humanity is so important.

Just in time, he feels. The phoenix unfurls its wings in front of him. It looks weak, but its will is strong. It had been dead for quite some time. Here is the revival of Nature, to reclaim what man has taken. The phoenix is the sign of the beginning and an omen of the end. He smiles. It is time to leave.

The phoenix is in skyward ascension. His eyes follow its path, eventually disappearing amongst the palette of grey above. The colors of the phoenix blend in without even shifting the surrounding shades, such careless grace within intuition, so instinctive and innate. Its cause of revival, known, but its effect, yet to be seen or felt. The echelon of what may come centralizes over his head. It can be felt in the bitterness and unconscientiousness of the rain, amiably meeting any surface with an alluring and ardent welcome by the triteness of this somatic realm of actuality.

The ocean plays an intimate melody, heard through the gentle swaying of lucidity and placidity, extracting his attention away from the skies above to command the most direct way out of the forest as his next steps of progression and consecution.

Though the path before him radiates with ardor, his feet weigh heavy as the clouds of insecurities that shroud his vision. She is within his grasp, but the distance between his trembling fingers and her transient hair is as vast as the oceans that he has called home. Lull, breathe, escape. His body trembles from a lack of cohesion, a frustration as pure and cohesive as his surroundings, a lack of color, a deficiency in his mind and all that is around him. It all makes sense, every note in this cacophonous tragedy has been accounted for, accentuating the highs and lows of his channel thus far, but how? He struggles to distinguish the beginning and ending, what has yet to become a part of his past and what has befallen him. His head spins in the same motion as the record on the phonograph, the scales of the serpent engraved upon the ouroboros marked deeply in repetition by the needle, creating a rich dissonant aria to serve as the backdrop to the chamber music that echoes within the hollow confines of his bewildered consciousness. The phonograph plays freely, the fine point tracing over the same route, always leading him to the same memory that he has become latched onto. Between the acute, chiseled needle and the untouched, virgin surface of the record lies in dormancy the distance that separates the waking and sleeping, the ambiguity that comes from both states of consciousness, the portmanteau between two worlds, beginnings and endings, and everything within and throughout, the soliloquy that resonates amidst the conscious and unconscious, as clever as the fox that outsmarts the wolf, and as unadorned as the brevity that the audience has expected, yet begotten. A separation that no human emotion could ever parallel. The unreal overwhelms what is perceived to be real. All he knows and understands could be mere constructs fabricated out of fragmented landscapes in lucid illusions alluding to times, events, recollections, and altered realities that have occurred or are yet to, an oscillation between the dimensions and the dimensionless, the thin line between existence and unreality, with measurements calculated through the swaying of consciousness on trajectories undetermined.

Chapter Twenty-Three
Circuitry

Embedded in the digital landscapes that define the endless borders of the mind lies the sedative, a creation, an algorithm formulated within one's own cognizance with the inclination and capacity to meld the human senses into a single rung of a ladder initiated from the top in the conscious world, culminating into downward steps that end far below the subconscious, a realm populated with times past, where recollections create the structures that are planted, roots firmly ingrained within the celestial terra firma, as the formation of impending rationalization shapes all that has yet to be materialized. The beacon outstretches its reach across every frequency, wavelength, and sensory pathway, traversing the desolate, surreal manifestation of an infinite mural with an endless horizon, beneath in the subconscious and above in the conscious.

Chapter Twenty-Four
Treachery of Thoughts and Transitions in Vespertine
Dissolution

Memory, a harbinger of how the future will be seen and felt. Memory, the most callous of mistresses. With one sullen sway of her fleeting shadow comes a wave of longing and reminiscence that crashes in unison to construct a circular, structural brink that imbricates upon the present moment without respite. Abstract, as if the past itself creates a threshold, a boundary of finite measures, every-changing, every-evolving, resounding in a piercing silence, a deafening frequency, drifting indistinctively amongst the winds that push and pull upon the highs and lows, the ebb and flow of the pendulum of three brief moments on a linear ladder of time. The past, the present, and the future, all encompassed in a singular consciousness, as unique and solitary as the emotions and recollections that arise from diacritic experiences shared in physical, material embodiments, but desolate in the ethereal moments afterwards that flee as swiftly as they came. As sure as the endings and beginnings of seasons, memories are created, harbored, protected, and cherished. As sure as the peaks and valleys of growing and withering, such memories fall deep into a recess or illuminated to bask in the glow of prominence within the present moment. But her, except her. She is the only constant in his mind, not time, not the gradual inclination of the brief sense of reprieve in the brief time span of life. It is her, it will always be her. She is, and always has been, and will be, from now until infinity, the beginning and the ending, the alpha and the omega, the nucleus of his life, with every memory of her in mind and in heart to strengthen her presence in his foundation to be carried out through means of existing within and without his mind and body. In a cognitive sense, she is time, merely a measurement of events between days and space passed. Beyond such measurements of moments and numbers, she is the reason for existence, a singular life force, and he James Covington, the parasite that feeds off of the presence left behind in her radiant wake. Recall and cherish the late-night musings over recollections, hazy, unclear, and imperfect, like cold rain on a summer day, where memories become mile markers on a lone highway through one's consciousness. The end? There is no end, just a mere constant progression of entries written in ranges of human emotions to be chronicled in sequences arranged in a sporadic manner dictated under the dominion of unmitigated bereavement and rapturous pleasure. Colors bleed from between the cracks in an unending sky, filling in blank shapes and contours with strokes from the palette, where the grey and the white release their grip on an infinite sky of memories repressed. Shades and spectrums begin to overwhelm and breathe a relieving life into melancholy through an aura of becoming and dissolution of the monochromatic still frame embedded in an ever so timely manner in the circular sequences of chronemics and happenstance. So take comfort in what has passed, though it may be the singular entity purely responsible for much of an unbearable misery and insurmountable joy, for it is what defines and molds much of the physical realm and also what lies beneath in the domain of repression, a perfect sphere of steadfast reasoning and hindsight as clear and pure as crystals. But break away, despite the comfort of the shackles around the limbs, despite the intrinsic value behind conformity and subjugated by crystalline deception. Lift the veil, awaken, to the breaking of restraints barring progression, the chains of consciousness shattering under the pressure of the strength to live, the dominion of recollection, fortuitously meandering in reverie, contemplating the next destination that has already been foreordained.

Chapter Twenty-Five
Anabiosis

He walks along the edge of the cliffs, contemplating what's below. One step in a divergent direction and his entire existence up to this focal point along the spectral timeline redirects to an alternate tangent. The end. What an anti-climatic ending, he ponders. The answers that he has sought, could they be below? Will the questions be unveiled as his listless, bloodied body lies barren on the throne of stones, bereft of the last breath in his swollen lungs, soon to be replaced with the fluid in his veins and the salt of the ocean? Will the questions that brought him to this moment fade to irrelevance, distortion, and inanition? If he chooses to move forward, mindful of his steps on the edge, how much further will he have to go? Contemplation ceases his physical movement as his conscience ponders the burden of the weight and destination of each foreseeable decision. All plausible, realistic, viable. His eyes close as he draws in what may very well be his final breath. His mouth agape from exhaustion without tangible progress. His heart beats to the rhythm of the waves upon the shore, the carefully articulated visceral and audial opera of the assimilation of an imminent death and an existence continued. The salt of the ocean will cleanse all wounds. This is it, this is it. Now or never. The wind wraps its fingers around his feet, an ethereal push closer and closer to an ecstatic free fall.

You are so weary, come sleep with the setting sun.

He feels a stringent sensation. The waves open their arms below, beckoning his body and mind to meld with the realm of Nature. The sound of eternal bliss is overwhelming. His mind, blank. An unmarked canvas of delicate beauty. The bitter poison, the sustained tarnishment of existing in such a world is extracted through his mind by the euphoric syringe of Nature and order. The syringe is drawn, as steady as the pendulum that sways amongst the waves. Ebb and flow. Fall away from this existence.

Chapter Twenty-Six
She

I still see her. Not on the same level of existence, but she is there. She is in another time, perfectly still, painting pictures of our lives, dreaming of me, my hands placed perfectly in hers, together. As do I. She is the brightest star, a mannequin of memories, a safe port in the most somber of storms, all mine, contained within one. She moves in grace, cutting in and out of various spaces and times, always burning a hole through the reels of the film that's played perpetually in the theater of my mind. The memories of her are as powerful as the love we had once shared. Some nights, I believe in fate. I believe in a predestined set of milestones that are realized as a passerby as a simple "I told you so," from a first-person perspective in an introspective reckoning. Other nights involve my hands molding and crafting a world of my own, the sovereignty of what I'd allow to become my past, curating this present, waking moment, and interweaving the fabric for the archetype of the future. What happens next in an immediate sense and what may come in the future rests invitingly in my embrace, with care and utmost articulation over how I perceive what lies ahead and beneath the perfect vision of what is present and what has passed from the eyes, but not of the eyes of the mind and inner perception, and repression. Some nights, I can live in pure bliss knowing that she will forever remain in a perfect state of equilibrium in a silver lined shroud and shrine of photographs, and amongst other nights, as restless as my heart and mind, I cannot help but to feel that the best part of my life has retreated from the frontlines of the war of an unconditional love to the background of a fading and failing play in the theater of chronemics and chronology. Yet, I still see her.

Chapter Twenty-Seven
Further

Be still. The familiar warmth of the sound from the record player gently streams into his consciousness, its melody engulfing his body, intoxicating his senses, warming his limbs, awakening his mind, unsewing his eyes wide shut. The hushed harmony on a constant loop, never reaching an end, never finding a beginning. At what point did it interweave with the fabrics of his consciousness to form an entire paradigm of memories based upon strings of tones, rhythms, syncopations, to rest within the cradle of benign suppressions that openly embrace the brightest and darkest recollections of his past that he wishes to forget, but will never want to forget? Coalesce, converge. There is no past if it's as present as his presence is in his meticulously crafted spherical world, with no set beginning that memory can offer and no end that his eyes have yet to perceive. All is now, all is today, this very moment. One foot in front of the other. Pure progress to process and progress the antithesis of regression, to aid forward thinking and perpetuality in a perfectly linear formation towards an uncertain end, a cloudy ocean of fate swept tenderly by the winds of manmade choices and idealized guises and hooded costumes of fate that dance discretely within the ballroom of the holy matrimony, the indecent, yet expected propagation between mankind and Nature. As fate and choice conjoin hands in eternal bliss and unrest, their celestial steps make waves upon the floorboards amongst the narrow aisles in synchronized unison. The triptych glows radiantly upon their newborn child. Mankind basks in its luminosity. Thus, the cradle of mankind is nurtured and the branches from deep within the ground slowly penetrate the surface, the outer layer of consciousness housed within the simplistic, logical mind of the individual as a whole. Layers upon layers of the roots burgeon throughout the roads of the mind, until its interconnectivity reaches a full revolution, where the beginning of thinking inevitably becomes the end of reflecting. The mirror's musing.

Consciousness regains control of the reins to the chariot of his senses. The tattered leather of the harness, blistered by the heat of the sun and drenched by the sweat of his brow and salt of the ocean, exert pressure downward on his feet, meddling with ghostly gravity. This is not the end. There is still much to do. The cliff's edge is tempting, its luscious lips whispering sweet nothings of a certain end, the terminus of physical and mental anguish. As seductive as the rumination may be, he knows that the waters below can only bestow a fleeting solace, an alleviation that would not bring him any closer to his wife and push him further form the answers that he so deliriously thirsts. He inches away from the ledge and back onto the path to Noumena. Though the road may seem endless, the progress and answers that are found along the way are markers of time passed that will eventually lead to the final destination that one has always longed for. Noumena, or the relics of it, awaits, and all of the secrets that the town had held for so long are manifested in a physical realm. All of the skeletons are out of the closet, awaiting a proper burial and ceremony by fate, choice, and time, the eternal judges and rulers of mankind. The clouds are painted in a darker hue over Noumena in the distance. Strikes of lightning adorn the picturesque painting that the town itself has composed with the palette of dissolution and eternity. Clamorous claps of thunder in the distance add a welcome change to the monotonous symphony of rainfall. As troubling as the skies above Noumena may show, it radiates an amorous glow that's as benevolent as the town itself in the past. All was well then, all will be well in the end. What reason is there to return to Noumena? Clouds connect like constellations in his mind, clouds as dark and thick as those above. There is no longer anything worthy of recollection there, yet as sure as gravity, it compels him to come closer to its center, to reminisce over its melancholic surroundings, a subtle, uneasy reminder that the town, like the melody of the record player, is firmly embedded within every inch of his skin, hooked within every mile of his veins, encoded within every last strand of his DNA. James and Noumena, two as one, a beautiful disaster disseminated by time and civilization, and to be destroyed and reclaimed by Nature. His steps, though weary and hesitant, steadily and firmly trudge through seemingly endless puddles and thick, blackened mud. Upon a small hill, he stands and draws in a breath of familiarity of times past and present. Familiar landmarks regain shapes through the thick fog. The clock tower casts a peculiar light upon the surrounding buildings, its shadows in an unchanging, fixed shade of darkness, as dim as the neurotic space connected in oblivious suspension between memories near, far, and beyond. Noumena is upon him now.

Chapter Twenty-Eight
Alexithymia

The town welcomes every one of his steps that lead closer to its heart. The silent carnival of shadows and recollections grow restless for an arrival long overdue. The bronze gate in the middle of the path remains strong and unwavered as ever, its only flaw being the jagged rust of disuse and degradation by time. He wraps his hands around the bars of the gate, pushing the frames out of its permanent state into an untouched position. These gates have seen the rise and fall of the town that he has fostered since its birth. At this point in time, the gates themselves have become the portal to the past, a glimpse into the well of repression, where countless memories of the townspeople entwine within the structures that stand upon the soils of the Earth, with roots outstretched deep within to anchor the conquests and progress of mankind as a permanent embedding of triumph over Nature. Though what's created by man on the surface will fade, its importance will only be measured by the history of glory or infamy that it leaves behind.

Chapter Twenty-Nine
Death

Nature is a particularly ardent, somatic body that will excise the tumor that humanity has become. Its hands will dig into the soil of the Earth and uproot all that is manmade, scattering the ruinations across space and time, leaving only faint traces of its cherished memories and past importance in place for all in awe to revel in the immortality and celestial strength of Nature, the cruel mistress that will always remind humanity of how ethereal and transient its time and place within this prism of reality and prison of consciousness truly is. The foundations, the structural arrangements of the genomes of Nature, consciously create boundaries that surround mankind with false depictions of control and false prosperities, giving humanity an unnatural sense of domination over a dominion that it has no remembrance of ever controlling since the beginning. There was never a beginning, nor will there be an end to human kind's misguided attempts and erroneous reasoning for controlling what cannot. Noumena is merely an abnormality. Society and mankind are the viruses that Nature is staving off. Noumena, the mutation, a disease that will soon become eradicated. Humanity and its conquests are mere glitches and obstructions in the trajectory of the oscillatory physics of the pendulum of Nature in realms, both corporeal and temporal. This is the end.

Chapter Thirty
Life

With the rusted gates behind him, there is nothing to come between him and the town. There is a purpose to his steadfast footsteps, but the purpose is as fleeting as the last rays of sunlight upon his weathered skin on the day that his wife had disappeared. Nine months, two weeks, three days ago. It feels longer, it all has blended in. Time cannot be measured anymore.

A sense of what has passed has melted into his past, a circular, never-ending vortex of failed aspirations, wishful thinking, events deemed memorable, traumatic moments within his trajectory of time. Has it been that long ago? Despite the passing of measurable time, his wife is the only memory that has not faded, but has only become stronger, manifesting into physicality, bleeding its way into his Elysian field of vision. The melody of the record player entices the angels to outstretch their wings and arms and guide James towards the predetermined, final destination. As if there truly is a set destination for one's soul. Thoughts and memories that would have flooded his mind and clouded his judgment back then lay in comfort and peace at the sandy shore of his consciousness. This is not the end.

Chapter Thirty-One
Aphotic

No longer do the crashing waves perpetuated by the hands of his emotions and heart affect his astute movement towards an unknown but certain fate, a fate similar to that of Noumena. Memories have reconstructed this town, despite its aging foundation and deteriorated façade, and he sees the town as how it used to be. Though he knows in his heart that all he sees is simply a glimpse into the past, he cannot resist wallowing in all that was good and bad about Noumena. Before his eyes and mind could glaze over in cognitive dissonance, the ground below him convulses in an unnerving manner. The waves of the dark blue expanse sway in an unfocused, dizzying formation. The winds that were pushing against his back alter directions and grow stronger. This breeze is different. The air thickens as his breathing strains his lungs, longing for calmer conditions. The rain no longer falls from above to gently caress his skin, but rather comes down in haste to the sound of syncopated thunder and lightning that looms closer and closer with every inhaled admiration and exhaled concern. These weather conditions emit a sort of felicity, a disparaging sense of calm that's suitable for what's to come. The waves separate, revealing an abyss as dark as the souls that used to inhabit Noumena. The blackest of unfulfilled desires, the deepest of repressed secrets, all brought to the port of neurosis, manifested from unadorned thoughts of obsession to material composites of sinful, human behavior. The town's secrets are no longer safe. All is exposed. Barren, virgin flesh for the first time feels the unfamiliar touch of mankind with all of its discrepancies, wickedness, and sins, unbeknownst to all that only encounter and meddle with the outer façade of a town that basked in superficiality and desacralization. This is the beginning of unbecoming.

Chapter Thirty-Two
Ruination

Dread emerges from within, tying his stomach into knots of discomfort and fear, a feeling of familiarity blended into the vast uncertainty of the unknown. From the spiral of the ocean below, a surreal sight. An array of grey teeth rises, accompanied by a worm-like body of riveted glossy skin. Discs upon discs, connected by transparent blood vessels and muscle tissue that steadily grow out of the abyss of the ocean, its mouth forming a vortex, changing the direction of the breeze that gently placed its lips on the sweat of his brow during every step on his journey thus far, slowly sucking in the paint and loose pieces of the structures that surround him. He plants his feet into the dirt, careful as to not let the wind push him closer to the enticing abyss at the center of the sphere of gnashing teeth. The sea worm erects its cylindrical body upwards, as high as his eyes can see, and for what felt like hours, its head remained in the clouds, as if devising and exacting a cruel and impending judgment on the town below. Come what may, Noumena is ready for its standing ovation. Relieve this place of its misery, the agonizing act of remembering the past in its most intricate of details and intimacies, where nothing but pain and melancholy adorn the foundations and structures of moments and memories, forever fleeting on the wings of borrowed time and the ocean's breeze. There is nothing here to be saved.

The colors that were once splashed upon the physical structures begin to fade, being stripped of any former recollection within one's mind. Pillars, as strong as the memories housed, waver in fright of erasure from the realm it had occupied. Darkened hues of rust and neglect peel and falter, effortlessly fading into a welcome reprieve. The paneling of the buildings, slowly deforming, lifts from its hinges in a delicate manner. The fingernails of Noumena are immaculately extracted. A prolonged but binding torture, the begotten conclusion, the final act in the tragedy of Noumena before the withered curtains fall and the stage that the town had once called home is dissolved into the soil, the weathered skin of the Earth. Noumena is being absorbed back into the ocean, a reclamation brought forth and meticulously executed by the elements that swallow humanity in time. Palettes fade slowly into the shades of what Noumena used to be before civilization, a beautiful spectrum of Nature. In a mere instant, the wind against his back gains the strength of a storm as the skies above bleed into heavier hues of grey. He struggles to hold onto a nearby tree, one that oddly waves in a delicate elegance, immune to the ravenous unbecoming of all that is manmade and superficial. The suction of the sea worm grows stronger, slowly inhaling discolored chips of paint and rotten fragments of wood, only leaving behind the skeletal remnants and cages of what once housed the individual and collective recollections of a town that mankind created and the terra that mankind enslaved. All that is stripped is taken to the clouds, disappearing behind the veil of sight within a tenebrous gloom.

Then silence. Quietude so static that the world stops for him. His inner monologue brought forth and explored verbatim by the intrigued, eager audience. Contemplative complacency and bewildering reverie wrap its wispy fingers around all that is beyond his physicality. Everything is embraced. Everything is innocent. Everything is discordant. This is the unison, perfectly imperfect. Not a single breeze could be felt upon his skin, or a drop of rain from above. Fragments of flesh that covered the breathing buildings float in hushed suspension. Beads of mist sail in place across his shrouded field of vision. The endless allure of solace in placidness lasts but a fleeting second, though the sensation is eternal.

As abruptly as the soliloquy of a silent fisherman commenced under the spotlight in the theater of euphoric repose, the head of the sea worm cascades over the vestige of Noumena, restless in its urge to uproot the town and its harbored memories without the contrition of retrospection. Its incantation proves to be a ballast of the ballad of wanton destruction, reigning unconditional power and control over the weakness and delicacy of the exploits and advancements endeavored by the human race. Time, devourer of all things. This is the end that is predestined for Noumena. The stillness that surrounded the supposed permanence of all that sails upon the breath of the ocean gratingly regains momentum towards the cylindrical, infinite depth within the creature's salivating orifice. He braces his body and mind to withstand and endure the test of looming catastrophe. Physically, he feels the strain, the pull towards a certain end, the fate that he could meet in this exact, transfixed moment, so long as he lets go of what keeps him grounded, palpably and obscurely, even to him, the pier of preservation of secrets and regrets. His fortitude from within ascends like a phoenix, the counterweight to align the physical inclinations of ephemerality. Though this compulsory extraction of the somatic structure, with its wicked tale of time elapsed, defines the destiny of Noumena, he is adamant to not be assimilated into such analogous fate. Stronger now, extraction is nigh. It takes an exhaustive amount of vitriolic time to unhinge what was, an outright erasure of all that was misguided since the inception of Noumena. The material world can only plant a seed so deep until it sprouts with deceit and malevolence at the tips of its archetypal branches. Extract the seed. Extract the inessential. The soil of the Earth that had once cradled and heightened the screams of humankind and society's pomposity of dominance will cave in to conceal and decontaminate the influence of such nefarious source. The wretched vultures of inevitability converge over the ravaged carcass of the town, fervently clawing at what remains. Their appetites of gluttory seek atonement and redemption for a sense of purpose in the poisoned well of their existence. The vultures pace back and forth between the ruins, contemplating whether they had had their fill of vile constructs and tasteless memories. Their eyes, full of galaxies between the beginning and the present, fall upon the bacchanal affair that stands in the vicinity, a gentleman of uncommon knowledge harnessed to the wings of the proverbial phoenix in ascension. This one ought not to be devoured. Time will tell his fate. The vultures spread their diseased wings of obscure banality and spiral skywards to become splotches of paint across the canvas above, the masterpiece by an artist unknown.

The highest reaches of the paradise above, the lowest fathoms of the inferno below, both extremities thrive on a cognitive complexion, a labyrinth void of an exit, a beginning and an end. Memory, the bane and blessing of existence in a tangible world. Its chronology in scattered chaos, a universe of specificity shining like a dull star upon a collection of moving images that had permeated within, and ultimately latched onto the narrow fibers of consciousness that flows through every vein within the physical self.

Away with thee, for time
is of one's own design.

While reasoning and consciousness seek to find an order within the chaos through chronology, the moments of living that fill the spaces between are unmeasurable, deemed unworthy and left to unbecome as a shunned, somber soliloquy to be auditioned for recollection in the times to come. The only member of the audience in the theater of cognizance awaits amongst the vast emptiness with utmost patience as the narrator of the events in inquisitive recollection murmurs a string of letters with forced meanings that cascade from a stream of consciousness to fall on the deaf ears of the physical world that lies outside. Beyond the walls of the theater, the limits of one's own mind, the burnished cogs of the machine of enslavement emit the precarious siren of familiarity, the unnatural order of chaos that mankind has created and sanctioned as the circumstance of a pretentious society.

Chapter Thirty-Three
Culling

Escape. There are no survivors in the end. The first step is oh so prodigious, unveiled with elegant cogitation, a favor presented in secrecy from above and below, in exact alignment with the linearity of time and consequence. Allow your weary, hesitant step to follow the one siren that lusts over your body, pleasuring herself to your stagnation or dissension.

Stagnation is the consummate cog in the machine of the perpetual inferno.

Dissension is the dilatory commencement of the revolution from within.

Which siren would you follow? Both are elegantly exquisite, with flaws and imperfections shining brightly in hues of black and white, eager to take your hand to opposite ends of the spectrum of what it means to be alive.

Chapter Thirty-Four
Constellations

Chaos subsides. All the world is calm, idle, a silence as deafening as the ghosts of the past, a piercing scream heard clearly through the lowest of frequencies, frequently pervasive in the darkest corners of deprivation and recession, an ephemeral threat that endeavors to wade through the subconscious stream that leads to the surface where the bronze machine of a fabricated society dictate and uphold the definition and constitution of living and breathing. To intrinsically erase all trace of Noumena would require a certain passing from this current physicality to a transient state of unbecoming to propagate the release of all that has kept the lucid mind and listless body in chained suspension. Noumena is the ghost that haunts him, walking in his shadows within every waking moment of consciousness, anxiously pouring the vitriolic poison in his glass every night until forced slumber, forever ensnared and enslaved by the melancholic reverie of diseased memories lifted from the poisoned well of subconsciousness. Without recollections, attachments, structures, chronemics, Noumena is but a destitute shell, a carcass picked clean and tempestuously polished by the gnashing of teeth by the intangible predators of fate.

Silence. Eradication. Abolishment.

The keys were in his hands this whole time. The textures, a
liquid form, lost in his grasp, void of edges and shadows,
molded perfectly to his palm, transparent and weightless, as
lucid as fleeting dreams and forthcoming nightmares. The fine
line that separates recollection and destiny merge callously,
where what has been has yet to occur, where fate flirts with the
anterior. His hands burn from the touch of what once was, his
conscience staggers and falls into a series of mechanical echoes,
mere visual glitches in a sequence of perpetual temporality
manifested within the infinite boundaries anchored within his
mind. In a pensive manner, as gentle as the breeze that cradles
his skin, enlightenment. Human, sans constraints, alive at long
last on wings of the continuum, with progression embedded
within the footprints that he has left behind, to a destination
subconsciously known, yet distant to the senses.

A ligneous door appears, standing in solitude amongst the
lonesome field of green, its composition a testament of stolidity,
upright as the strongest of structures, weathered by the
unforgiving hands of Mother Nature. Its placement in the
vacancy beckons his inquisitiveness, drawing his body closer to
its physical façade, sparking the wonder within and the
bewilderment of the unknown of what lies behind the door. As
the sounds of silence steadily grow louder with every movement
towards the curious aberration before him, his hands begin to
waver, with fingers grasped tightly upon an object unbeknownst,
unfamiliar, surreal. The keys in his hands gravitate towards the
lock on the door, a consummate pairing, a cathartic unison.

Unlatch. Push through. Awestruck. The mind wanders over
miles of wonders.

He stands confounded over the sight. What used to be miles of
rocky shores with abandoned, anchored boats resting on the
darkest of sands has become a dune of the silkiest of white,
windswept sands that protrude from beneath the waves of the
ocean itself. As hesitant as his next steps are, the curiosity
emitted from the vast unknown draws him in through the door.

The archaic frame of the door begins to dissolve into an intangible distance that only time could measure, into a recollection of a time that had transpired, relapsed from the past to this very moment to serve a fruitful purpose to his bacchanal desire to satiate his lust for the arduous search for something that never was, until it never was not. As impalpable as what's before him may seem, he feels her allure, her aura immured upon every fragment of space within and without the discoloration contrary to what he beheld to be absolute at one point in a time irrevocable and irreversible.

Chapter Thirty-Five
Searching

We are all ghosts, physical, yet intangible, past, yet present. What has passed, despite chronologically dwelling in the past, is as present as what's presented when eyes fall upon the presence, the ghosts of connected memories, the sorrow behind regret, the bliss within romance, the malevolence of the unknown. The past is alive in one's mind, with memory reshaping and recreating a projection until it's vivid enough to bring forth the other senses that were lost in that moment, to replay and relive the opulent scene on the vacant stage of the mind. Moments are never lost, but float freely within one's consciousness, above and below, between waking and sleeping, forever expansive, forever infinite.

Chapter Thirty-Six
Veneer

Beyond the effervescent structure of memory, beyond the frail grasp of recollections, a monument stands as infinite as the horizon, a natural wonder that emits a shade of the painter's palette that is brushed upon the barren terra in stark contrast to the liquid oblivion of the ocean that beckons him closer with every exhaled breath. The road reaches its end. The world opens and the only sounds heard are those that he creates and causes. His eyes take in as much as possible before blinking, knowing that should he close his eyes for long, he may not want to wake. The grey skies no longer exert an impending fate. They lay dormant and docile, pinned above him, almost as if the veneer has been shed, its ashes floating effortlessly towards the grounds of stability to converge once again with the Earth, thus completing its own circle of transgression, regression, and progression, as brought forth and taken away by the perpetuality of time. The winds that effortlessly sail across the waves find themselves being guided by invisible hands that row over the treacherous highs and confounding lows of the dunes of the desert that span to the edge of his sight. The clouds kiss the rays of faint sunlight as they caress each other's ethereal beauty, falling upon the soft sheets of the desert to create and give birth to a splendor that overwhelms the senses, drawing the breath away from those who stand and bear witness. All sign posts and road markers will eventually lead to this place, where time is not defined, where memories are not formed. The sand is undisturbed by footsteps, just the natural peaks and valleys created and shaped merely by the soft, gentle fingers of the wind deep within the warmth of the sands. The silky breath from the lips of the breeze flows freely through his hair, sweeping over the curvatures and contours of his body without the faintest effort. His walls collapse, he has never felt so free. His mind attempts to determine the effect he would have should he disturb such tranquility. He carefully places each step on the sand as if it were the shards of glass that used to line every inch of his wooden floor. The sand shifts, opening a warm cradle for his limbs, eagerly waiting and moaning for the presence of something that has not touched this virgin land. Euphoric. Ecstatic. There is no dissimilarity within the reflection of nature upon the mirror of all that the eye can perceive. The lush complexions that mix amongst the tips of the bristles paint a perfect composition in one color, in one stroke of the wrist of the musing artist. The painting is removed from its easel, and in one fell swoop, dropped upon the land below, and as gravity draws the drawing closer to human perception, the hues and shades are brought to a vibrant life, with each shade complementing its negative and positive attributes until our eyes can only see the beauty and wonder of how a simple, minimalistic painting can alter and shape the contours of the physicality that humanity perceives and exalts. In the distance, a lull, a wandering voice of melancholy and curiosity, a siren, piercing but in a way that the composition of the ballad of the siren calmly smothers to sleep the sounds that aim to be heard by him. The notes serpentine through the chasm of nihility and entwine around every movement he makes across the dunes. A gentle push, a timely essence, the dune's lament over the end of purity and innocence, as he stands on top of the peak, eyes as wide as his mind can be, drawing in every shape from the sight and pitch from the sound until his canvas of the wonder in front of him is the masterpiece that he has desired and sought all along.

Chapter Thirty-Seven
The Penultimate Paradox

At the end of his journey, the ocean. At the beginning of his doubt, a pier leading to an island. He doesn't recall seeing this pier before, and the island? Unknown. A malicious, yet affable glow radiates from the fog that encircles the island. The tops of trees mark the apex that looms above the ring of grey, harboring all that lies beneath and within its shroud. It's merely another mystery to unfurl and reveal, fear has no place here, yet leaving without uncovering the possible spring of elation or fountain of despair is not an option that he ruminates over as his body moves against his idle resolve, closer and closer to flirt with the outer edges of the monument. This is the swan song of searching. Lunar, solar. Cycles that have run its spherical course end and begin again. It's a soothing sensation knowing that this neoteric relic that lies before him is the finale of his symphony. The bittersweet symphony that glides over the silky sand is orchestrated with a fervent reminiscence, amidst the dissonance that still holds an affinity for the past and its destructive complexion. Sail across the sand on the crusade of spiritual and physical augmentation. Let what has passed fade away, for the past fails to be of any abstruse significance at this destined station. His heart is open, ready to be revived by the hands that inscribed the final notes of the rhapsody of his soliloquy. Lift the curtains of premonition, close the curtains of doubt. It's within arm's reach, the reason he still breathes.

Chapter Thirty-Eight
Cadenza

This euphoria of unknowing, the oblivion that rests as a burden
of fallacy or veracity on the threshold of the contemplation that
results from the ambiguity of life and death, a passionately
fulfilling life or a slowly realized death by the dispassionate
hands of time until decrepitude or a slight squeeze of a trigger on
a loaded gun to one's temple, are all merely products of the
control that's imposed as a feeling of choice dictating the actions
taken in every passing, dispassionate minute seen passed on a
fabricated, mechanized clock that a supposed advanced society
of a divided, broken humanity lustfully created to dictate,
manipulate, and ordain the illusion of control, an allusive morale
that comes with the brief right of existence before passing on to
what may or may not happen afterwards, where one's belief of
what comes next is the most plausible and logical outcome, an
unbalanced state where perpetuality and singularity converge
and are derived from one source within one's mind in one
occurrence, either random and chaotic or systematic and stable.
But as of late, skepticism shrouds the confines of his mind,
where questions and deferment, as tangential as they are, recede
further and deeper from an illuminated annotation. Who is to say
that he is alive to begin with? What if his mind and the minds of
other humans, and the complexities that befall such minds, were
mere hallucinations of one core system that perpetuates a
movement of existence disseminated upon all that lies within
and beyond the singular, eccentric composition only understood
by the composition and its tangents of logic and improbability
through introspection? Oh, but the retrospection! An inert,
ravenous oblivion incessantly masticating on the mind and soul
of a sole human bereft of a cohesive pattern within varying
tangents to form a model of a purported life once lived. As
irrational as it seems, it seems coherent, given the time, space,
and circumstance that materialized before him. So is this the
moment where he is fully alive? Awakened from a drowning
drone of death with a single spark of what feels to be redemptive
in reasoning in motive. So he must've been dead this whole
time, or, for a more fascinating take, perhaps in a coma?
Floating freely through levels of dimensions at ease, at peace,

oblivious in oblivion, whether it has been for the past nine months, or for his whole life, but what difference would the length of time make? Living, dying, and transitioning through stages and levels in the same theater that the mind occupies, regardless of whether an audience is there or not, is left to his own vivid interpretation and lucid imagination. Is there a singular absolute to enshrine within the temple of the body and sanctuary of the heart? Maybe so, maybe not, but as far as he knows, this is the moment he's been living and dying for. The pier and his wife.

Chapter Thirty-Nine
Projections

Upon birth, the moment one's eyes open is the creation of a universe and the unbecoming of the previous. The parallel divide between fabrics of time and contours of physicality are torn and stitched in such paradoxical mirror images that a blank slate that is yearning for existence becomes specifically that, a blank slate. Such chaos and disorder amongst a beautiful birth, proportionately balanced, like being and its parallax. Unitary knowing and vacuous unknowing converging to begin and end the process, onwards to an influx of flashing lights amongst an array of shades. Boundless depth within images transpire themselves upon the virgin periphery. Echoes, bleeps, and drones of varying wavelengths rain heavily upon a landscape of purity. Nerve endings spark and react, gazing in awe and bewilderment over what it could have been that led to their awakening. Time, the immeasurable kind, flies. Lines and arcs meld to form a complex system of entwined sounds that purport labels with characteristics based upon a mere five senses, and environments and surroundings become metaphors of perceptions of reality. Yet she remains, in a stillness that would baffle physics and Nature, not as a chemical hallucination within the mind, but more as an undefined object of permanence, as essential and vital to life and death as a conscience or oxygen, an imagination or water. She is there, dimensionless and endless, perpetual in her lucidness and corporeality. His footsteps make haste, gaining a momentum that hasn't been witnessed in his odyssey thus far. Her silhouette begins to illustrate sharper curves and features, protruding from the backdrop of somberness and brooding despondency. Her smile is all he longs for in this moment, to make sure that it still is as alluring, magnetic, and tender as how he remembers it. Gravity is of no burden, as his body naturally flickers through space and time towards her delineation written in blood by his reminiscence. She directs him through the ridges of sand to a set of stairs, leading up to the discordant planks of a decrepit pier held together by the premonition of the coalescence of their eternal love once more, under the slight auspices of an imagination that defies the outline of the archetype of actuality and abstractness. The whole world stops. It's him and her now, and this moment was worth the most astringent of struggles, and the traversal of misery and infernal nightmares, feats that he would undergo over and over, for her, for her love.

Anything and everything for you, my inamorata.

Her smile shines, as illuminating and radiant as how he blissfully remembers, her cascading hair gently caressed by the faint, placid breeze of the ocean and an audience that applauds the convergence and harmonization of two souls that were destined by fate and choice to be as one. He smiles, the sight of her, the sweet traces of an amorous perfume that elicits memories of the best of days when they would spend innumerable hours gazing within the nebulous skies, thankful for each other and the love that they share, and for the safe harbor that they've created within each other to withstand the darkest of times and the most restless of storms that may permeate or erode their essence and love for one another.

His arms extend outwards to lull her into his eager embrace, releasing the emptiness that he has kept captive for so long, a friend, a ghost, a figure with an obtrusive definition that has kept him in a balanced state of constant pessimism and optimism in his fruitless but redemptive search for meaning without a clear definition or form, a paradigm hidden in the antithesis of progression and constancy and elucidated premonitions of instances predetermined. As close as his fingertips will allow, as close as the ends of her flowing hair permits, the closest they have ever been, quite literally a love and bond that crosses the threshold of all known and unknown boundaries, is where his next journey begins.

Her silhouette and enchanting scent drifts from his proximity, leaving a transient trail of ghostly wisps that beckon him to slowly cross the bridge to the other side, where the island lies listlessly in a reflective solitude, desperate for his physical enthrallment and arousal of bewilderment that has remained an enigma since his hollowed eyes peered through the drudgery of materiality and preclusion of reclusion that rests anchored to the delusion of incisions upon the aperture that inhales the mediocrity and falsity that has proven, and continues to, negate a will of absolute freedom without a malignant leash of ascendancy held rigidly in the vice grip of an assured fate and precarious choice.

The potent poison of memory begins to bleed from his skin, an anomalous thread as thin as hair, as light as air, as frail as the vessel it had occupied, slithering towards the purity left in her wake to create the toxic unison of her fate and his choice. The wisps of his past are extracted calmly, and the euphoric sensation beckons him to bridge the divide between his concerted immersions with her seraphic warmth. Then, a tension that has riddled him throughout his existence begins to lift. It abates a thought that has haunted him for so long and a brief recollection of the introspection flickers in his eyes as they fixate upon the object around his wrist. It is no longer there. So he follows, regardless of what may come, though in his heart, he knows that this is destined, as well as how the ending will transpire, the final reel to be projected, the final sentence to be written, the final breath to be drawn in. Steady steps begin to resonate in tune with the waves gently crashing beneath the wood, the echoes of an impellent furtherance of a man no longer bound to temporal constraints and confinement, no longer ravaged by the anguish of anamnesis.

Converge.

Chapter Forty
Transgression

The slight taste of the bitter salt of the ocean that lines the inside of his mouth attenuates to a state of insipid suspension within the opening. An essence that he has known for his whole life, vanishing as swiftly as his reaction to its diminishment, but at this point, he cannot turn back, never to contemplate the progress made so far, and the unforeseen distance he has yet to traverse to reach the desirous end he has yearned for. The water of the ocean that has kept him alive for so long, the water in his canteen that has kept him alive for so long, its element, the elixir, its purity on his lips, gone in the blink of an eye, in the delicate passing of eager footsteps across the pier. His mind wanders for a moment, thoughts upon thoughts as to how and why his sense of taste has been afflicted. The drunken revelry, the hasteful liquid of suppression ingested in excessive amounts, its taste, no matter the bitterness that has latched onto the series of recollections, no matter the flavorful sweetness of his wife's lips flowing abundantly in the period of time before the architect of self began to construct a destructive, hollow, and crestfallen shell of a man in the face of a calamitous tragedy, the dissolution of a human being and the perpetual agony of the scars of an awakening realized and contemplated. As much as his memory begs of him for a release of remembrance of what the salt tasted like, his cognition says and proves otherwise, with austere focus wholly fixated on what lies at the end of the pier. Proceed to the propagation.

Constant uniformity of the stentorian waves underneath culminates to create the harmonious accompaniment to his wayward passage. The smell of the ocean is seductive, tempting in its lament for his return, far from land, away from humanity and cultural advancement, a dominion where his mind can augment and reconnect with the apex of oscillation within the sphere of the emulous individual hidden within the trite collective. The dunes behind him appear as rustic landscapes, runes of materiality unbeknownst and virgin to an error, a human tangent yet to be materialized and introduced as an axiom of transcendent propagation, standing feebly before him as admonitions of his journey thus far and of what's to come. He begins to notice that the air he draws in lacks the aura of the ocean below and before him. It dissipates whimsically, as if he is traversing towards the antithesis of his perennial reprieval of fortitude and repose, though at this point on the pier, his physical shell closely resembles a gravestone indolently positioned between at what may quite possibly be waking and sleeping, life and death, Heaven and Hell. His recollection of the ambrosial serenity slowly slips away from the roots in his mind that entwined such scent to the ravishing veneer of an inveterate romance with the ocean, and with the postulate spiraling downwards to a vacuum of connections faltered and memory delineated to a monotonous innocence, lucid and undiminished, his state of reminiscence propels itself to an imbued relapse of an undisclosed symphony, sympathetic to those that have lost the sense of admiring the ensemble, callous to those whose fingertips have callused from the edges of the unhinged pages of notes and melodies performed indifferently to the eager advocates and apathetic antagonists of the winds of vicissitude and foredestination. And change, without caution, as alacritous as the doves of a reality fully realized loosened from captivity, came swiftly with a frigid, detached welcome. His sense of smell has gone astray.

An analysis at this point is overdue, but to overanalyze a predicament that's as chimerical and perplexed as the one he is unwillingly participating in is merely a paradox of stagnation, where the movement of time and the physical self is at a standstill, unsure of a defined direction. He grows desirous of lucid explanations and a sense of progression as a unison of puzzlement mystifies him, where the pieces of the anagram emerge as shapes of a spherical nature without a set allotment, a Gordian knot crafted by the capricious hands of destiny and the enduring human will. Further now. His hand glides along the wooden railing, free from the splinters of times past, exonerated of the indignation of the sun's rays, second only to an unconditional absolvement of the scourge of existence, hidden with the minute granules of sand in the chromatic hourglass of life and time elapsed, and amidst pensive pertinence, memories of days in shades of sepia and nights in façades of black and white cascade over the monarchal structures in his mind with ease. And then, a brooding numbness, as persistent and delicate as inertia, exudes from within and throughout his limbs, bereft of admonition, ominous in its demeanor and deficient volition. The planks that have supported his stride thus far begin to lose their rigid luster, instead giving way to an obscure perplexity of walking on air without corporeal exertion, the unequivocal movement now a mere series of perpetuality and disorientation. Odd how transparent prevalent actions become devoid of credence and conscientiousness once the inherent nature of perception is distorted by an anomalistic hindrance. His hands ardently pace their way back and forth across the wooden railing, desirous of any vestige of feeling, but as postulated, nothing. His breathing frantically intensifies, but bears no burden on his lungs. He raises his hands, bloodied from splinters, disheveled from the dirt embedded within the moist wood, and yet, despite the palpable reaction to seeing such entropy unfold within his hands, there is no pain, nor mourning, but only a diaphanous, somber catharsis of the sense of touch.

In retrospect, his appetence for insight, knowledge, and answers, through judicious gallantry, had brought him this far, and turning back towards the dunes at this foreboding moment would be an attestation of his repression of an apprehension of what has transpired, the matter at hand, and what lies ahead. The rune rests within the ruins of his past and of what has passed, an allegorical rumination, a fractured remembrance of times past, immediate, and expired, permeating through boundless dimensions and tangents birthed and ravaged by the individual's singular, spherical consciousness. The temptation is overwhelming, as the unknown void that remains after each step towards the island mystifies every sense of reason and rationality, contorting and averting every connotation of what has been affixed and perpetuated by a fabricated prison within a prism for a human race led astray by the apparatus of our own making since its genesis. As his eyes close to inhale the lifeless air into his capacious lungs, the void of perception begins to escape from the coiled corners of his vision. His eyes flicker in horror, burning with ambiguity as his sight, once so full of luster and color, begin to collide with the greyness of the skies, a blinding fog of an unclear spectrum that emits a paralyzing, somber sensation, melting into a blurry, amalgamated haze, evocative of the painter's palette that had once adorned the celestial sphere. As the last of the dying light fades from the outer surface of his desolate, withered field of vision, he draws in a breath as deep as the ocean below, as if he were to fall through the uncharted continuum with no hope of ever rising to the surface again. Alas, a world of darkness, underwater in the fathomless depths of an objectified inferno, silver lined with a frigid coldness that accentuates all that glitters in the warmth of the light that's narrowly escaping the darkness dwelling in the shadow of his past and present self. Wander through the darkness and ambiguity. All that remains is his hearing and an austere, straightforward path to his intimate terminus. His steps are lethargic to take heed of his body's adjustment to the sudden affliction of blindness, yet the direction is as incisive as it has been and ever will be.

Fall away, a strange, new expanse welcomes his presence, where the only predictable paradox is his hearing and the absurdity of communication, though at any moment, such paradox could also become a variable to be factored out of the equation of corporeality. It is an enigma of existence that one takes for granted, especially when the sustained notes of the tune emitted from the record player is a rich, bountiful reminder of his delicate yet hardened past, a past that he would go to the ends of the horizon for, all to keep the nucleus of recollection from falling below the threshold of memory into a perilous oblivion, only to be conjured in wisps in passing of moments impetuously repressed, torn asunder, or merely forgotten. In a vibrant, pitch black stasis, his steps wander in unison in the purported direction, without hesitation, without weariness. His shoes, worn from the journey, create a familiar sound as it settles upon the weathered wood below, and just as soon as the contentment of conversance consumes his body, it's heedlessly overtaken by a fractured, discordant melody, as loud as it has ever been, a lucid signal towards or away from a perennial misery he has endured thus far. His imminent haven, delineated and measured in the resonance and ardor of the melody towards what he has longed for all along, inches closer in tonality to pure auditory dissonance, a vividly intricate blur of a cacophonous orchestra that strings together the final words and breath of a melodic threnody and a solemn eulogy of enlightenment and martyrdom. Wander, in darkness, on a progressive trajectory. The melody, with every note and tone, is blended into a singular mixture of a peremptory realization that this ceremony is merely a physiological transformation further towards a rational regression and a perennial progression. His arms give into gravity, languidly subsiding to his sides. Despite a scarcity of sensation, his mind is resolute that the manifested destination is looming. The light and dark in his dimension, as seen through his vacant eyes, coalesce, caving in to an endless euphoria beyond what he could ever elucidate through articulation. His hearing, forsaken and dissolved, now solely a distant hum of a memory. Collapse. His hands and knees connect and embrace the remaining number of timeworn planks to crudely bisect the distance between what's behind and before him. A change in perspective, a change in perception. The skies above, through the omniscient overcast, cast their blessings and judgment down upon his ailing cage of existence as it crawls through the skin of an environment that was entwined and embedded within his physiological system. Alas, his steps reach the end of the pier on to a different consistency, as marked by the concluding lamentation of deliverance from all that has transpired. His body trembles, his legs give in, his eyes darken. Destination, realized. Clarity, found.

Shed this veneer and unravel.

Chapter Forty-One
Consummation

Repent, lament, collapse before the impending cataclysm, pray and prey for a sweet release from the vice grip of treacherous recollections, for there is nothing left to miss, nothing left to fear, nothing left to search for. Parallels collide, horizons converge, the end begets the beginning, fate and choice focalize under the scope of the oceans above and the skies below.

Was it worth it? It always was, it always will be. No matter how fleeting the sense of time was in my dreamscape, no matter whether the temporary reprieve of seconds/minutes/hours from a callous heart was worth the recommencement of a light/mild/heavy depression, weighing as heavy as the heart in the morning, or as light as the smile she carries in my vision when my eyes shut, it will always be worth the acquirement of that one still frame of her, where it soars far beyond mere reels being replayed, but more likely a tangent of another life, another life with her once more, where we create a new landscape where we are so in love with each other, the way it used to be, the way it should have been.

Crystalline vision has led to complete transgression. Undress the regression of all human traits, rewrite the rebirth of the protagonist upon a tabula rasa. Incisions, held loosely together by the sutures of the perceived, fragmented reality, begin to exude the consummate elixir of the uncharted, an axiomatic sensation of drowning and helplessness in one's own abyss. Then, there remained a mass of clothes, the vicissitudes of time and seasons throughout the years had left their imprints of intangible materiality upon the frayed fabric. Bone, blood, sweat, flesh, gone with a halcyon fragrance of his reverberant past seeping through his clothing, liberated into the ambience of the theater that he had embellished for all of his life. Alas, the epiphanic respite, the celestial transmigration. She smiles, reaches for his sweaty, diffident hand, and calms his restless heart, leading him out of the light, through the darkness. The most befitting ending transpires amidst the resounding reveille of ecstasy and paradise, at long last.

It's as if he were dreaming.